FROZEN MUSIC

The Harper Short Novel Series

———————————

FRANCIS KING

FROZEN MUSIC

ILLUSTRATIONS BY PATRICK PROCKTOR

1817

HARPER & ROW, PUBLISHERS, New York

Cambridge, Philadelphia, San Francisco, Washington
London, Mexico City, São Paulo, Singapore, Sydney

To

KAY DICK

For Gallantry

Allen County Public Library
Ft. Wayne, Indiana

FROZEN MUSIC. Copyright © 1987 by Francis King. Illustrations copyright © 1987 by Patrick Procktor. All rights reserved. Printed in the United States of America. No part of this book may be used or reproduced in any manner whatsoever without written permission except in the case of brief quotations embodied in critical articles and reviews. For information address Harper & Row, Publishers, Inc., 10 E. 53rd Street, New York, N.Y. 10022. Published simultaneously in Canada by Fitzhenry & Whiteside Ltd., Toronto.

FIRST HARPER & ROW EDITION 1988

Designer: Lydia Link

Library of Congress Cataloging-in-Publication Data

King, Francis Henry.
　　Frozen music.

　　(The Harper short novel series)
　　I. Procktor, Patrick. II. Title.
PR6061.I45F76　1988　　823'.914　　87-45631
ISBN 0-06-015875-1

88 89 90 91 92 MPC 10 9 8 7 6 5 4 3 2 1

ONE

7153155

*I*T WAS KIRSTI WHO FIRST NOTICED. It was late afternoon and the sun was slanting through the tattered, dusty trees on the western side of the road, as though through slats. In the parallel bars of illumination, the air seemed thicker and heavier, not, as in temperate climates, clearer and lighter. We were approaching a town, with factory chimneys coughing up smoke in the distance and, above them, a sky streaked with a metallic orange. 'Oh, look, look!' she cried out, as she had so often cried out to us when we had passed something that had delighted, appalled or amused her.

But it was too late for my father or me to look. The car had rushed on, seeming now to soar up effortlessly into the air and now to plunge juddering and jarring into an abyss, with the dust raised by its passage billowing behind it. My father stirred, opened his eyes and put up the back of a hand to wipe away the thread of saliva dangling from his chin. 'What, what?' he asked, with the fretfulness that, usually so even-tempered, he showed only when roused from his sleep. 'What's it this time?'

Kirsti leant forward, putting one of her strong, competent hands on his shoulder with obvious affection. 'I saw something so strange. Could I have imagined it? I saw a board by the roadside which said "Welcome to Balram".'

'It couldn't have said that. We're nowhere near Balram. I'd recognize it at once if we were.'

'Well, that's what I'm sure it said.' She laughed. 'We've talked so much about Balram. Perhaps I've had a hallucination.' She once again leant back against the cracked upholstery beside me. In that slanting light her Finnish hair, bleached by our long days out in the sun, looked almost white. I thought, not for the first time, how beautiful she was, and how lucky my father was to have married her when he was sixty-one and she, only three years older than myself, was barely thirty.

But it was Balram. Hanging askew on a crazily buckled fence, behind which I could glimpse what appeared to be the Victorian Gothic edifice of an institution of some kind — school, business headquarters, government office? — there hung a board on which, as we rushed on, I could see written 'Akbar Inn', under a picture of a square, porticoed building, with a semicircular drive before it. 'Look! Look!'

'Is this Balram?' my father turned to Rajiv to ask, in the gentle, indulgent tone, as of a father to a spoiled child, that he always used to him. Anyone else of that age, after all those hours of bumping along largely unmade roads, might have been sharp.

'Oh, no, sahib. Not possible. Balram is far to the west, sahib. When we return, we return via Balram. This is not Balram, sahib.' But I was at once certain, from the ashamed, fearful way in which he gave his answer, that Rajiv already knew that it was Balram. Not having my father's sweetness of nature, I wanted to shout out, 'Oh, for God's sake! Can't you read a road sign or a map?' But I restrained myself because — I realize now, although I did not realize it then — I did not want

Kirsti to make unfavourable comparisons between my father and me.

'We had better ask someone,' Kirsti said. Then, because the Indian gave no indication of having taken this in, she leant forward, putting her hand on his shoulder with the same affection that she had shown when putting it on my father's. 'Rajiv, be a dear — ask someone.'

I knew that at that moment of humiliation Rajiv momentarily hated us, as he slowed down the car and brought it to a halt outside a wayside kiosk where, shaded by a ragged thatch of palm leaves, a group of men were squatting or sprawling on a platform, tin bowls of food and tin mugs of tea before them.

They all shouted at once, some of them even gesticulating. It was clear that, yes, this was Balram.

'This is Balram, sahib,' Rajiv said to my father in a low, tremulous voice as though he were confessing to some crime.

Kirsti laughed, her teeth white in her sunburned, healthy face. 'Then what are we doing here, Rajiv?'

'Oh, it doesn't matter,' my father said — quick, as always, to protect anyone whom he felt to be under attack. 'The boy made a mistake, that's all. Wrong turning, something like that.'

Rajiv looked simultaneously grateful to him and miserable. 'Yes. I made mistake, sahib. I am sorry, sahib.'

My father patted his knee. 'Not to worry. Mistakes occur in even the best regulated of households.' I winced, as I always did when he brought out, as though he had just minted it, some worn and tarnished cliché. He shifted and straightened his body in his seat, and then began to peer first ahead and then out of the window beside him. 'Strange,' he said in a bewildered, even apprehensive voice. 'It's so unlike what I remember. I might be remembering some totally different town.'

'Well, it's almost twenty years, father.'

'Yes, almost twenty years.' He sighed, as though for the loss as much of my mother here in Balram as of the place that once the two of them had known.

'Things can change a lot in twenty years,' Kirsti said.

'They can, they can indeed.' My father's eyes were now fixed on the white road ahead of us. No doubt he was pondering the changes in his life that had taken him from his years of vagabondage in India back to the war in England and then on to his career of publisher of art and academic books.

'Since we are here, would you like to go to the cemetery now?' Kirsti asked.

'No, no, no!' My father cried out the words with the incipient panic of a patient who, expecting to be taken to the operating theatre on the following day, suddenly sees the trolley approaching his bed. 'We'll go there on our return, as planned. We don't want to arrive in Indore too late, and we don't want poor Rajiv to have another drive with all those unlit bullock carts and all those people wandering about in the middle of the road.'

'All right, darling.'

The road had now improved, its asphalt no longer so ruinously fissured and pitted. But because of the indifferently straying pedestrians, cows and pariah dogs, the flimsy, crammed auto-rickshaws, the dust-streaked buses with people glued to their outsides like flies, and the constantly hooting cars attempting to pass us in the face of other constantly hooting cars, our progress was much slower. I seemed to be seeing everything through a film of dust raised by the traffic and of smoke belching out of the starkly utilitarian factory chimneys on either side of us. The same sense of oppression overcame me as when we alighted from the car and there immediately, all around us, were hordes of crippled beggars, screeching pedlars and importunate children, jostling and plucking at us.

'What a hideous place!' Kirsti exclaimed, gazing out of the window beside her. 'I think the most hideous we've seen so far.' She touched my father on the shoulder. 'Philip — I thought you said Balram was *attractive*.'

Slumped in his seat again, as though he had once more fallen asleep, my father replied in a low, discouraged voice, 'These are the industrial suburbs. When one leaves them behind, one sees the real Balram.' I knew that he wanted to believe this but was only half able to do so. 'But of course the place has changed, as the rest of India has changed. It has become less and less of a rural economy.' He turned his handsome head, too large for his compact body, as he often did in the car when, in the manner of a benign schoolmaster, he was instructing us. 'When the history of the twentieth century in India comes to be written fifty years hence, I think it will be generally acknowledged that Birla, the man chiefly responsible for industrializing India, was a far more important figure than Gandhi — who, incidentally and, some might think, symbolically, was assassinated in the grounds of Birla's house. Gandhi looked back to the spinning wheel, the bullock and the hoe. Birla looked forward to all we see around us.'

'So much the worse for Birla,' Kirsti remarked.

We had now been obliged to halt behind a long queue of vehicles at a hand-operated railway crossing, on either side of which red lights flashed on and off through the murk of the early evening. Clearly everyone around us — the man, in turban and flowing robes, who managed to remain balanced on his bicycle only by leaning one elbow on the side of our car, the women with huge earthenware or tin pots on their heads, the diminutive child leading an emaciated goat — was returning home from work. Far off I could hear the train. Its rhythmical pounding grew louder and louder. It passed with a long-drawn, slowly diminishing shriek and a billow of dark-grey, sulphur-smelling smoke. I remembered then that Balram was an important railway junction, and that my uncle, my mother's brother, had been managing director of the railway when it was still privately owned and still British. That was why my mother had died in this place.

'I look forward to a bath and a drink,' my father said.

'You could have a drink now,' Kirsti said, as a bent, stiffly moving man — he looked far older than my father but was probably far younger — effortfully wound up the railway-crossing gate and the queue began to nudge forward. 'There must be at least one Martini left in the thermos.'

My father shook his head. 'No, I'll wait, thank you.' The various small rituals of his life had their fixed hours. A Martini was something to be drunk before dinner and perhaps even before luncheon, but never at any other time.

'What about you, Rupert?'

I shook my head. 'I'm feeling thirsty. A Martini will only make it worse.'

'Sure?'

'Absolutely.'

'Oh, good!' Kirsti began to unscrew the top of the thermos. 'Then I needn't feel any guilt at drinking everything that's left.'

Rajiv looked over his shoulder. 'Do you wish me to stop for you to have some juice, sahib?' he asked me.

'No, we'd better push on. The more one drinks in this heat,

the more one sweats. And the more one sweats, the more one drinks. It's a vicious circle.'

It was then that I saw it. Kirsti did not do so because she was tipping back her head, the cup of the thermos raised to her lips. My father did not do so because once again his chin was on his breastbone and his eyes were shut. We had passed a sprawling factory, grey under a grey sky, with all about it huts, made of wood or corrugated iron, which in Europe would have been regarded as habitations fit only for animals. Outside the huts women squatted before charcoal fires, preparing the evening meal for the menfolk now coming home. The smoke from the innumerable fires joined the smoke from the factory chimneys to soil and blur everything. Beside the road, between a petrol station, with a number of dusty, antiquated trucks stacked before it, and a restaurant, with a neon sign capriciously flickering 'Rajput Brasserie', there was an elaborate wrought-iron double gate, one side of which was open. On the side that was not open, I could read the word 'Cemetery' in Gothic lettering. Above the 'Cemetery', there was a rusty Gothic cross.

I have often wondered in the twenty-five or so years since then why I did not call out to Rajiv to stop or at least rouse my father to tell him: 'We've just passed what must be the Christian cemetery.' I think that my own shock at the cruel disparity between what I had expected and what had been revealed restrained me from inflicting an even greater shock of the same nature on my poor father. That he would inevitably have to endure that shock in due course on our return to Balram was something that I was either too foolish or too cowardly to take into consideration.

'Are you all right?' Kirsti, who had now drained her Martini, was looking at me with concern.

[13]

'Yes, of course. Why?'

'I don't know. You look – different.'

It was, of course, not only I but the cemetery, momentarily glimpsed through those high wrought-iron gates, that looked different.

As a boy of eight, I had not been taken to my mother's funeral, much less to her burial, so that I had never seen the cemetery for myself. But my father had so often spoken about it to me and even to Kirsti that I had in my mind what passed for a vivid recollection. It had been only the evening before, as we had sat out under a full moon on one of the terraces of the island Lake Palace Hotel in Udaipur, that he had yet again reverted to the subject. 'I can think of no more beautiful place in which to be buried. One goes out of Balram some two, perhaps three, miles, by this dusty, unmade road that passes through what is more a little settlement than a village. The road winds up into the hills, and there, on the slope of one of them, is this cemetery, with not a single dwelling in sight. Someone at some time way back in the nineteenth century erected some wrought-iron gates extraordinarily pompous for a place so small and simple, and someone, more happily, planted trees and shrubs. There is a well in the middle, and the gardeners draw water from it to ensure that everything is always green.' He raised his tankard of beer and gulped from it. 'There are these graves going back to the time of the old East India Company. Graves of officials and soldiers and businessmen, graves of young women who came out to get married and at once succumbed to cholera or typhoid or malaria, graves, oh so many graves, of young children. Heartbreaking, those.' Again he gulped from the tankard. 'Well, you'll see for yourself.'

'You must be happy that Irene is buried there,' Kirsti said in a soft voice. It always seemed to me an indication of her essential decency and goodness that whenever my father reminisced about my mother, she showed none of the exasperated jealousy of most women in such circumstances.

'Yes, I'm happy Irene is buried there, indeed I am. I sometimes think that's where I'd like to be buried too.'

And where is Kirsti to be buried? I wanted to ask of this man who, although naturally so kindly, could so often inadvertently, as now, be so brutal.

My father had a way of repeating some favourite recollection over and over again, in the same hypnotically vivid way, so that in the end what had been his experience also became mine and would, in the years ahead, also become Kirsti's. I could see that white, dusty, narrow road, now a crowded thoroughfare, winding up into an increasingly green landscape. I could feel the stone of the parapet around the well, abrasive on my palms as I leaned over and gazed down, down, to where, far below me, the previously stagnant water had been shattered into splinters of light by the stone that I had tossed into it. I could hear the dry clatter of the cicadas about the gravestones, with their marble or granite crosses, angels, scrolls, bibles. I could smell the roses that, years before, had been planted by obedient gardeners under the stern directions of some memsahib, parasol held open in one hand above her. I could share in the grief of my father, as the Canadian missionary — Mr Vellacott: I had always re-membered the name — had read the service in a nasally resonant voice and as, the service over, the half-naked Indians standing by had picked up their shovels and begun to shower earth down upon the coffin. My father had made me a present of what had been the most profound experience of his life, just as he had made me a present of so many more trivial ones.

'You're very sombre,' Kirsti said, with her uncanny ability to guess at the moods of others.

'I'm tired,' I said shortly.

'We seem to have missed the really beautiful part of Balram.' My father had again turned round in his seat, a hand resting on its back.

Kirsti laid her own hand on top of his. 'Yes, we must have done. All this is awful, awful. How could your brother-in-law have borne to live here?'

'Oh, one had to put up with a lot in those days,' my father said.

He himself had had to put up with the death of my mother when she was only thirty-one.

TWO

'MOGUL TRUST HOUSE FORTE,' my father muttered, his open-necked shirt hanging out of his baggy and creased cotton trousers, as he insisted, to everyone's embarrassment, on carrying his suitcase for himself instead of leaving it for one of the horde of sleek boys, in red uniforms picked out with gold braid, who crowded the concourse.

On the veined red marble slab, the colour of a slice of raw beef, of the reception desk, a notice announced 'Mr Gerald Singh' and, under that in smaller letters, 'Assistant Manager'.

Mr Singh, whose complexion was the beautiful colour of an ivory cigarette holder faintly tinged with nicotine and who wore a shimmering grey silk jacket buttoned up to the neck, had a disconcerting way of letting his melancholy eyes wander to what appeared to be someone standing just behind me, a little to my right. But when eventually I looked over my shoulder to see who kept attracting his attention, there was no one there.

It was my father who invariably decided our itineraries, as was perhaps only right since, out of the modest fortune inherited from my mother, he was paying for both Kirsti and me. But if the itinerary was his, it was I who was expected to realize it, poring over timetables and guidebooks, haggling over charges, or, as now, arguing because we had been told that something that we had long since booked was not booked.

'I am sorry, sir. Very sorry.' Mr Singh did indeed look very sorry, long, upcurling eyelashes lowered over those melancholy eyes. 'You may see for yourself, sir. I am not kidding you.' He turned the ledger round to me. 'You will see for yourself that we have no such booking entered.' It was, in fact, impossible to see for myself, so quickly did he jerk the ledger back again.

I went over to where my father was slumped in an armchair. Kirsti stood beside him, cigarette in hand. Beyond her, I could see our luggage, neatly piled onto a trolley from which it would now presumably have to be unpiled. Beyond the trolley, Rajiv was peering in through the glass revolving doors, a hand shielding his eyes. No doubt he had been put off entering by both the opulence of the lobby and the condescending self-importance of even the humblest members of the staff.

'Well?' Kirsti asked. She knew that I hated these confrontations. But she also knew that, since I had accepted this role of courier imposed on me by my father, it would be useless for her, so much better equipped for it by temperament, to offer to take it over now.

'No rooms. He says he knows absolutely nothing about the reservations. Unfortunately that girl in the hotel in Bombay never gave us any kind of written confirmation.'

'Always get a written confirmation,' my father muttered. He smiled up at me, to draw the barb from the implied criticism.

'Since the same group owns both hotels, I never thought . . .' Then I lowered my head to him and whispered, even though Mr Singh was too far away and too busy with another customer to hear even my normal voice. 'Perhaps a present might help?'

'Oh, no, no!'

Foolish of me to have said that. When, three days before, I had made the similar suggestion of a 'present' after it had become clear that we were not going to get a seat on a plane for which we had been short-listed, my father had given way to one of his rare attacks of anger. 'In a country in which visitors like us hold all the financial trumps, it is wrong for us to use them to take local people's aces.' I had refrained from pointing out that I had just seen an elderly woman in a sari, innumerable broad-banded rings pinching her plump fingers, slipping the equivalent of a trump of high denomination to the booking clerk, at once to receive one of the boarding passes previously denied to us. Had I done so, my father would have regarded it as yet another example of the cynicism of which he so often, albeit always so gently, accused me.

'Then what are we to do?'

'Oh, we'll find somewhere else. In a town as large as Indore, there are bound to be any number of hotels.' As always in these crises, Kirsti was reassuring.

I returned to the reception desk, where Mr Singh looked up from the English-language newspaper now spread out before him. 'Yes, sir?' We might never before have spoken to each other.

'Are you sure you can't fit us in somewhere, anywhere?' But already I knew the futility of my pleading.

'Sir, I regret. But, as I have already told you, the hotel is full. We have a party of Americans coming. Many people.'

'Can you recommend somewhere else?'

'There is the Lantern Hotel, sir. Not as modern as this hotel, not air-conditioned. But it is a good hotel.'

Hoping that my father was not watching me, I furtively drew a note out of my pocket and pushed it across the counter. 'Do you think you could telephone the Lantern Hotel for us and ask?'

Mr Singh looked down at the note between us as though it were one of the cockroaches that are ubiquitous in Indian hotels even as new and as clean as this one. Then he picked it up with an air of faint disdain, opened a drawer in the desk, and dropped it in. He crossed over to the telephone.

The Lantern was also full, with another party of Western tourists, this time French. Mr Singh was clearly not prepared to telephone anywhere else, since two luxury coaches had by now drawn up outside the hotel, to disgorge a number of middle-aged men and women all seeming to wear exactly the same kinds of sun hats and dark glasses. The boys were officiously crowding around them, some of them even struggling to relieve the new arrivals of handbags or camera cases which they were fiercely determined not to give up.

'I will take you,' Rajiv said firmly when we explained the situation to him on leaving the hotel. Two of the boys had reluctantly abandoned the Americans to heave our luggage back into the dust-streaked car.

'You know of somewhere?' I asked.

Rajiv nodded. 'Nice hotel, sahib. Not far from here. Near to palace. Clean. Cheap.'

The boys, having finished their task, were now awaiting their tips. Kirsti opened her bag and gave each a note. Then she gave me an apologetic glance, conscious of having usurped my role.

'What are we waiting for?' All my father's former weariness and despondency had left him. 'Let's go there.'

The hotel was called Ritz Garden. But there was no sign of ritziness, other than a tarnished brass vase containing a single artificial rose on the reception desk, and no sign of a garden other than an expanse of yellowish-brown grass between the dilapidated red-brick building, with its steep gables, and the noisy main road. At least rooms were available, a single for me and a suite — it was all that was left, it would be a little more expensive than a double room, the manager explained — for my father and Kirsti.

My father now broke into the negotiations between the manager and myself. 'What about our driver?' he asked. 'You have somewhere for our driver?'

'Oh, yes, sir, certainly, sir.' The manager, who was short and plump, the front of his white shirt stained with curry, had none of Mr Singh's elegance. But I thought that he would probably prove to be kinder and more helpful.

'Put the cost of the room on our bill, of course,' my father said. From time to time Kirsti or I would remind him that our agreement had been that we should pay for neither Rajiv's lodging nor his food. But my father would not listen. He turned to Rajiv. 'This gentleman will find you a room. A nice room.' He smiled at the manager. 'Of course we'll pay for it.'

'Oh, sahib, that is not necessary. Please, sahib.' Rajiv was distressed — or put up a good show of being so.

'Nonsense. That was a long, long drive over difficult country.'

Rajiv put his palms together before him and bowed his head, as though my father were some god to be thanked for his munificence.

I had been feeling depressed ever since I had had that glimpse of the cemetery under the intermingling smoke of the factory and of the charcoal fires outside all those hideous little dwellings scattered around it. Now the room into which the manager had shown me intensified that depression. Small and square, it had high walls, with a single window set so near the stained, cracked ceiling that I could not see out of it even by standing on tiptoe. There was an iron truckle bed, with a single threadbare sheet covering its lumpy mattress. Although freshly washed, the pillowcase had a meandering, curry-coloured stain on it, like that on the manager's shirt. My examination of the adjoining bathroom was equally discouraging. The lavatory bowl was blocked up with beige, shiny paper, similar to that on the roll that lay, soggy, on its side in a puddle at its base. The rose of the shower dripped water with a melancholy lisping.

We had agreed to meet for a drink in the suite just as soon as we had had our baths — in my case a euphemism — and unpacked. Having refreshed myself under the shower, turning this way and that to catch its trickle of lukewarm water, I suddenly felt a desire to know what lay beyond the window. I could hear women's voices, high-pitched and excitable, and the screams of laughter that constantly punctuated them. I could also, from far off, hear a dog barking with desolate persistence. As soon as night began to fall during our Indian travels, there always seemed to be some such dog.

I pulled the only chair, a straightbacked, cane-seated one, from beside the bed to under the window, and then, in nothing but my pants, climbed on to it, paying no heed to its wobbling and creaking. The window, I discovered, was not so much a window as an aperture, with no frame to it, let alone panes of glass. I peered downwards. There was an irregularly shaped area of bare ground, on which about a dozen women, some no more than pubescent girls and some wizened crones, were squatting. Blackened pots rested above open wood and charcoal fires, which the women from time to time fed either by breaking up a stick of wood or by reaching for a handful of charcoal from one or other of the two untidy heaps in which they were piled. One woman, wholly absorbed in her task, was dismembering some raw meat on the ground, while another, having blown her nose vigorously on her hand, had begun to slice some giant onions.

Hungry before, I now felt no desire for dinner.

'Come in!' It was my father, not Kirsti, who called out at my knock. 'Kirsti's not quite dressed,' he explained. Through the door opening out from the dusty, dilapidated sitting room — 'These might have been the quarters of an Indian Miss Havisham,' my father later commented — I briefly caught a glimpse of Kirsti's back, totally naked but for a towel thrown over a shoulder. Hurriedly I looked away, not wishing my father to see me looking, and when I looked again she was no longer visible.

'The usual?' my father asked.

The usual was duty-free gin with the local tonic water. I nodded. 'Lovely.'

My father poured out the gin sparingly. When, in the aftermath of the collapse of my marriage, I had once again gone to live with him in his St John's Wood house — Kirsti and he had not yet met — he would often remonstrate with me for 'knocking it back' (his phrase) when I returned, tired and depressed, from the office. 'You're not becoming an alcoholic?' he had even asked me, more disquieted than severe, on

one occasion. 'No, father, I am not.' But, in fact, it was something that I had started to wonder myself.

'No ice. Kirsti rang the bell for some and then, when no one came, even went down in a dressing gown to ask that man at the desk. He said he'd send some up straightaway. That was at least twenty minutes ago.'

'Well, all the guidebooks warn one about the dangers of ice, don't they?'

I wondered whether to tell him of what I had seen below my window. Then, since we had decided to eat in the hotel, it seemed kinder not to.

Kirsti came through from the bedroom, fully dressed now but drying her hair on the towel that I had previously glimpsed thrown over her naked shoulder. 'What's your room like?' she asked.

I pulled a face. 'All right,' I said in the kind of tone that made it clear that it was far from all right.

'Poor Rupert. You always have the worst of the rooms. That's the penalty for being on your own.'

I smiled up at her. 'Not the only penalty.'

'Poor Rupert,' she repeated, throwing the towel over the arm of the sofa. 'Don't you wish you had our suite?'

I looked around the cavernous room, with its tattered red velvet curtains hanging askew from windows from which the wire mosquito netting had rusted away to leave innumerable gaping holes, its threadbare carpet, its sofa so broken-down that neither my father nor I had dared to sit on it, and its electric fan motionless above our heads, either fused or disconnected, since no switch would get it to start. There was an unmade camp bed in one corner. I pointed. 'I could always sleep on that. Looks more comfortable than the bed in my room.'

Kirsti laughed. 'Yes, why not?'

'Not on your life,' my father intervened. 'You talk far too much in your sleep.' Did I really talk in my sleep? It was something that he had repeatedly told me while I was living with him. No one, not even my former wife, Caroline, had ever made the same accusation. Perhaps I had started to talk in my sleep only after she had left me.

'Come and see the other rooms,' Kirsti suggested.

'OK.'

'Over here there's a dining room. So, if we wanted, I suppose we could have our dinner sent up.'

'To arrive as promptly as the ice.'

The dark, heavy oak table and the chairs that matched it must, I imagined, have been shipped out from Maple's or Waring & Gillow many years before by someone like my uncle. Perhaps — I liked the absurd fancy — they had indeed belonged to him. The top of the table was now scratched in many places, as though it had eventually been relegated to a kitchen. One of its bulbous legs had been clumsily mended with two splints of wood that matched neither with each other nor with the rest. On one wall there was a print of an ageing, pensive Queen Victoria, seen in profile, and on another a photograph of an obese Indian baby boy, lolling totally naked, his uncircumcised penis a minute tassel, on what appeared to be some kind of desk.

We went back into the sitting room, where my father was trying to read a guidebook, holding it up to the dim light disseminated by the few candle bulbs in the tarnished brass Edwardian electrolier above him, and crossed over to the door through which I had had that glimpse of Kirsti naked. The bedroom was almost entirely filled by a vast, sagging double bed, its head surmounted by a brass crown from which a

canopy of ragged purple silk tumbled in dusty folds. 'Isn't that something?' Kirsti said, pointing to it.

At all the hotels at which we had so far stayed, she and my father had had twin beds, as they had at home. Would they sleep here together tonight, side by side, shrouded, even stifled by that dusty canopy? Or would one or other of them use that camp bed, claimed by me in joke?

'And the bathroom's even more something. Look.' Kirsti opened the door to it. A vast bath, high brass taps at its farthest end, reared up on lion claws. The lavatory, raised on a dais, was like a throne, with a stirrup-like brass handle set into the mahogany of its surround, to be pulled upwards to flush it – if, indeed, it could ever now be flushed. Suddenly I saw, half by the bath and half under it, the brassiere. Another of the surprises that Kirsti had sprung on me on this trip – although I did not imagine that she had left it there purposely for me to see on my tour of inspection. Not the sort of brassiere that one would expect a woman of her kind to wear at that period, way back in the fifties; it might have come from some small, furtive shop in Soho, its windows full, among similar items of underwear, of boned stays, riding crops and perilously high-heeled boots.

We returned to my father, who looked up and said, 'I'm famished.'

'I seem to have lost my appetite,' I replied. Again I refrained from telling him and Kirsti of the scene of the women preparing food on the bare earth below my bedroom window.

Most of the tables in the cavernous, ill-lit dining room were unoccupied, even though they had all been elaborately laid. A handsome, sleepy young waiter, his turban askew and his long fingernails ingrained with dirt, roused himself and stepped forward from the wall against which he had been leaning. 'Good evening, sahib.' It was my father whom he addressed, ignoring Kirsti and me. Throughout our journey people invariably assumed, either because of his age or because of his air of quiet authority, that he was our leader. 'I have kept this table specially for you, sahib. Best table.'

The table was no better than any other table. And why should the waiter have kept a table specially for us, since we had given no indication that we planned to eat in the restaurant? But with his usual old-fashioned courtesy, all too often taken for irony by more sophisticated people, my father said, 'How kind. How very kind. Yes, I like this table.'

The tablecloth had on it a curry stain similar to those on the manager's shirtfront and on the pillowcase but far larger. Half over it, as though in a futile attempt to conceal it, there stood a tarnished brass vase with a single paper rose, like the one on the reception desk.

Kirsti ordered curry, as she always did, not because she liked it but because it seemed right to her to eat what the Indians ate. She smiled up at the sleepy-eyed waiter: 'But not hot.' She repeated, 'Not hot. Mild, please.'

'Not hot, memsahib. Mild. Very good. I will tell cook.'

I also ordered curry. My father, having stared for a long time at the vast, tattered menu, on which most of the items had been scored through with green ink, at last opted for fish.

The curry was so hot that, though I was able to eat mine, Kirsti had to make do with rice and dahl. My father sniffed at his fish, glistening before him in its misshapen cocoon of batter, black at the edges, and then cut off a piece and put it in his mouth. He chewed for a while. Then he said, 'I may of course be wrong, but I have a suspicion that this fish may have gone off.'

Kirsti grabbed his arm as he was about to cut off another piece. 'Then for heaven's sake, don't eat it!'

'I expect it's all right.'

'Let's send it back,' I said.

'Oh, no, no, I'm sure it's all right.' As usual, my father shrank from hurting feelings with a complaint.

Kirsti pulled the plate towards her and sniffed at the monstrous balloon of batter. 'No, you can't eat that,' she said with the calm firmness, as of a nanny to a child, that she occasionally – not often enough, in my opinion – used to him. 'It stinks of ammonia.'

'Oh, it's not as bad as that!'

'It was silly to order fish,' I put in, 'when we're so far from the sea. We'll send it back and get you an omelette or something like that.'

'No, no! We don't want to upset them. I'll eat these potatoes and peas.' The peas, clearly from a tin, were as large as haricot beans and a metallic green in colour.

'For God's sake, father! If they serve up food as bad as this, they deserve to be upset.'

My father shook his head sadly. I knew that it was useless to persist.

Above us, in the silence that followed, a fan creaked slowly round and round, nudging the recalcitrant air.

Then, suddenly, from a table behind me, unoccupied when we had entered, I heard a furious man's voice: 'What the hell's going on here? Is there no service? Do we have to wait all night?'

As one of the waiters, not the one who had been attending us, hurried across the room, I thought: *That's a voice from my childhood*. I had never heard my father shout at any Indian, however humble, like that, but I had heard my uncle and many of my uncle's friends and colleagues do so.

'I am sorry, sahib. Very busy tonight, sahib.' The waiter sounded abject. From my childhood I summoned up an image of a head tilted submissively downwards towards a far from clean napkin folded over an arm.

'If you don't get a move on bloody quick, I'll report you to the manager.'

I could not resist turning round. At the head of the table there was, to my amazement, not some puffy, crimson-faced relic of the Raj, but a beautiful young Sikh, his curly beard in a net. On one side of him sat an aristocratic-looking woman in Western dress, and on the other, also in Western dress, two young children, a boy and a girl.

I turned back, to meet my father's sad, reproachful eyes. 'Nothing changes. Christ said, "Rend your hearts, not your garments." What he might have said was "Rend your hearts, not your political systems".'

After dinner, our spirits consumed by the restlessness that is so often a symptom of being overtired, we wandered out of the hotel and down one narrow, ill-lit street after another. We knew that we should never get lost, since Kirsti has an unerring sense of direction, as if within her she carried a magnetic needle. Although it was not yet ten o'clock there was hardly anyone about.

'Fancy Rajiv recommending that dump!' Kirsti exclaimed.

'How can a boy like that know a good hotel from a bad one?' my father reproached her. 'One might as well expect that old chap there on that bike to know the difference between a Picasso and a daub in an art school. There's no frame of reference.'

I stared up at the mouldering façade of what must once have been a handsome building, perhaps even a palace. 'I expect he's hoping for a rake-off. Perhaps the manager or the owner is a friend.'

'Oh, no!' My father was shocked.

'Well, that's how things work in India, isn't it? The land of the bribe and rake-off.' I had felt an uncontrollable urge to shock my father even more.

'Rajiv's a good boy,' my father said quietly. 'He wouldn't do anything like that.' It both amused and exasperated me that he should so often use the word 'boy' of someone who, as he well knew, was little younger than myself and had already fathered two children. He would never have used the word 'boy' of me.

When we at last returned to the hotel, it was in almost total darkness, and the front door was bolted. I rapped on the door and then peered through one of its dusty panes of glass into the seemingly deserted lobby, a single light burning dimly. Again I rapped, this time more insistently. At last a night porter, in nothing but a singlet and a pair of baggy cotton trousers, his feet bare and his hair tousled, appeared from behind the reception desk, where presumably he had bedded down, and shuffled towards us, a hand rubbing an eye.

'Good evening, sahib. Very sorry, sahib. I was attending to something.' All too clearly what he had been attending to was taking a nap.

'It's we who should apologize for coming back so late,' my father said, even though he must have been aware that it was only a few minutes after eleven. Then he leaned towards me to whisper, 'Give him something. I've no change on me. I'll refund you later.'

I'll refund you later. Repeatedly I heard that sentence during our travels. Sometimes my father failed to refund me at all, sometimes he pressed on me a sum far in excess of what I had spent. Why in India did he experience this reluctance, as of some monarch, himself to handle money?

I slipped the man the few coins that I found in my trouser pocket.

That night I had one of those dreams from which one awakes with as vivid a memory of its emotions as of its events. I was making my way through the high, wrought-iron gates of the Balram cemetery, one of a crowd of mourners, behind a plain wooden coffin. The coffin was my mother's and I, a child of eight, had been allowed to attend her funeral, as I had not been allowed to do in real life. The cemetery was not that cemetery seen momentarily from the speeding car on my first adult journey into Balram, but the cemetery that I had first imagined, so many years before, from my father's accounts of it, and had then carried around with me as a constant, poignant memory.

All at once, with the inconsequentiality and illogic of dreams, no longer the child Rupert, I had somehow become my father. At that my grief became even more acute, a weight within me so huge and heavy that, in order to carry it, I had to bow over as I walked.

Again there was a transformation. Now it was my present, adult self who was walking with the mourners, and the body in the coffin was no longer my mother's but my former wife's. I felt none of my old bitterness towards her but only sadness, regret, longing. Slowly we made our way up the avenue of graves.

We were standing by a raw, red hole in the earth. As I stared down into it, I became aware of my father beside me, dressed not in black like everyone else but in the creased cotton trousers, linen jacket and open-necked shirt worn day after day during our tour. He was quietly sobbing. Where was Kirsti? In panic, I looked all around, among the blank faces of people totally unknown to me, for some sight of her until, in a flash, I knew, with the terrible certainty of dreams, that the body in the coffin, at this moment being lowered into that raw, red hole in the earth by two sweating, grunting, half-naked Indians, was neither my long-dead mother's nor my all too living former wife's, but hers.

When I struggled up into consciousness out of that abyss of horror, my body was drenched in sweat. Far off, the dog of the early evening was still barking desolately — or was it some other dog? A mosquito whined near my left ear.

Again I slept, and, as I did so, the same dream faded and returned, faded and returned, as the world around one continually fades and returns as one fights against unconsciousness. But the emotion of acute grief never fluctuated, a hard, throbbing core at the centre of all that was vague, misty, deliquescent.

Referred pain. In my state of half waking and half sleeping, the phrase came to me. *Referred pain.* Before we had left for India, I had had to see the dentist about a constantly nagging pain in my jaw. 'No, that's not the source,' she had said when I had indicated a tooth. 'In fact, it's a tooth on the other side.' *Referred pain.* The pain was there from my dream, so sharp that I wondered if it would ever begin to ebb. But whose loss was it that had caused the pain? From whom had it been referred? It seemed to me, in that grey, ghostly time before the dawn broke, that it was being endlessly ricocheted around and around and around between all three of the women — my mother, my former wife and Kirsti — whom now, in the

[34]

memory of a man approaching his sixties, I see as the most important individuals in my whole life.

What eventually jerked me up fully into consciousness was the chatter, punctuated by screeches of laughter, of the women at their work below my window. Presumably, although my watch showed that it was only a few minutes after five, they had already started on their preparation of breakfast. For a while I lay listening to them, my body at last cool after a night of sweating, and my mind, previously so restless, now at last at peace.

As, my arms straight to my sides, I gazed up at the ceiling, crisscrossed with innumerable tiny cracks, I suddenly saw, in one corner, where the wardrobe cast a shadow, a lizard no bigger than my little finger and a brilliant emerald green in colour. It was totally motionless but for the constant throbbing of its throat and an occasional shuttering of the mica of the eye turned towards me. Beautiful creature. It gave me a feeling of pleasure as acute as that derived from any of the temples, palaces, gardens or caves that we had visited, with my father lecturing us in his soft, courteous voice on their history or, craning back his large, handsome head, pointing out to us some detail that we must not, absolutely must not miss.

. . . Then, all at once, a small, sturdy boy, I was in my uncle's garden in Balram, wandering there disconsolate in the heat of the afternoon. My uncle had set off, on the trolley on which he would sometimes let me accompany him, on an inspection of the line. My father, who had breakfasted long before anyone else, was away on an expedition to some Mogul fortress — when he had told me about its history the evening before, I had merely pretended to listen, as so often in adult life I would merely pretend to listen, while my abstracted mind traced some labyrinthine journey of its own, of which he remained wholly unaware. Pattie, my governess — in those days she would have been described as a Eurasian, today as an Anglo-Indian — had the day off to visit her father, a driver on my uncle's railway (I always thought of the railway as my uncle's, even though he was merely its managing director), and that mother and those brothers and sisters of hers who spoke with a sing-song accent that I was not allowed to imitate even in joke. My mother lay in the room, curtains drawn against the sun and an electric fan whirring beside her, into which my father, my uncle or Pattie would sometimes lead me, but which I had been forbidden to enter on my own.

There was something ominous about the absence of all people, even the two near-naked gardeners, an elderly man and a boy, apparently his nephew, whom my uncle would describe as 'simple', about the silence broken only by the chatter or scream of some invisible bird, and about the sky which, hanging low over the trees, had the sort of bituminous sheen to it which, I knew, announced one of the ferocious thunderstorms of which my poor mother had such an unreasoning terror, cowering in a corner of a room or on her bed, her hands pressed to her ears.

I walked beside one of the narrow channels that crisscrossed the garden, bringing it water drawn from a well by a bullock constantly circling on the same narrow track, by way of a cistern near which I had been forbidden to go. No water now flowed through the channels but they still glistened with streaks of moisture like the tracks of snails. Mr Vellacott's son, Clive, with whom I had been used to playing, had left two days before for 'home' in the care of a friend of the family. Soon, my father said, when my mother had recovered enough to travel, I too would have to go 'home' to be 'educated' — apparently my lessons with Pattie were no kind of education. Apart from Clive Vellacott, there were no other children in Balram whom my uncle (I suspect that my father thought otherwise but, a guest in his brother-in-law's house, did not care to say so) considered 'suitable' for me. Certainly Pattie's younger siblings, with those sing-song accents of theirs, were not 'suitable', much though I longed to join in their raucous, rough games on the *maidan*.

Suddenly, there it was. Perhaps as the young man that I was on my return to Balram or as the ageing man that I am now, I should never have seen it, green against the darker green of the *neem* tree, but then I had a youthful sharpness of eye, which was later to enable me to achieve popularity at school as a games player, even if the academic distinction craved for me by my father was always to elude me. It was the same colour as the lizard, but this emerald, unlike the lizard's, was spattered with an orange of the same shade as those curry stains on the manager's shirtfront, on the pillowcase and on the hotel tablecloth so many years later. It, too, had a throat that throbbed in and out like a pulse, and it too, its head turned sideways, so that it seemed to be looking at me askance, showed an eye like a splinter of mica, to be shuttered from time to time by a pale grey film. Beautiful. I stood there, motionless and silent, in a state of bewitchment.

Then I heard a voice. 'Hello there!' It came from across the garden, where a pink gravel drive, swept and raked each morning by one of the gardeners, fanned out to the road. It was the young Canadian missionary doctor, Mr Vellacott's assistant. Lying on my bed, in the cool, grey dawn, I could not remember what he was called, and even now it is with an effort, as though I were trying to dredge some long-lost object out of a well fathoms deep, that I struggle to recall it. Yes, ah yes, Jack . . . Jack Mackenzie.

I turned my head slowly. I did not wish to make any movement or utter any sound that would frighten the tree frog (that was what, later, my father told me that it was). But even with that slow turning of my head there was a plop and it was gone, somewhere into the undergrowth of high, lacy ferns. I waved a hand, feeling at the same time both disappointment at the loss of the beautiful creature and exasperation with this man who was little more than a stranger to me.

'All alone?' He came striding across the grass. Then, with an easy athleticism, he leapt an intervening flowerbed, no doubt knowing my uncle's fussiness about everything in a garden that now, in my memory of my juvenile, not my adult, view of it, glows for me like some earthly paradise.

I nodded. I was not a child who ever spoke much, making people think, not that I was shy, which was the truth, but that I was unfriendly and sullen.

'This must be a difficult time for you.' He put out a large hand (years later, lying on the bed, I saw it in every detail, whereas the face remained a blur, however much I struggled to bring it into focus), freckled and thick with the same reddish-blond hair that, cut en brosse, also bristled up from his head. He placed the hand on the back of my neck and gave it a squeeze. How difficult the time was, since I had no inkling that my mother was dying, I did not then realize. 'Poor Rupert. It's a pity you're not allowed to play with other children.'

'I was allowed to play with Clive Vellacott.'

'Yeah, sure. But . . . Oh, well, never mind.'

In the late afternoon sunlight his shadow was immensely long beside my own. He was so much taller and broader than either my father or my uncle. I did not think that I had ever seen anyone so tall and broad, unless it was the tattooed, heavily moustached steward in charge of the swimming pool on our voyage out. 'Would you like to come back with me and listen to my shortwave wireless? You've never done that, have you? If we're lucky, we can get the news from England. We might even get the news from New York — or, or Moscow — or Berlin. . . . Yes, we might even hear Hitler ranting and raving. Not that we'd understand what he was ranting and raving about.'

'OK.' The proposition thrilled me, but there was no way he would have guessed that.

My uncle frequently expressed disapproval of Jack Mackenzie's bicycle. 'You'd think that either the mission would provide him with a car or he could himself afford to buy one,' he remarked on one occasion when, ourselves in the cumbrous chauffeur-driven saloon provided by the railway, we saw Jack zigzagging deftly through the traffic, the sweat gleaming on his muscular bare forearms. 'It's wrong for him to be seen pedalling himself about like some babu or box wallah.' On another occasion, inspecting the bicycle, which Jack had left leaning against one of the pillars of the grandiose portico of the house while he was visiting my mother, my uncle had shaken his head and said to my father, 'For God's sake, why does he have to ride a bike with those high, high handlebars? It makes him look even more ridiculous.' 'Well, I think he once told me he bought it second hand in the market,' my father replied on that last occasion, as though my uncle had put the question to get an answer. Then my father added, 'I don't think he cares about dignity, do you?' It was clear that my father, unlike my uncle, did not think dignity to be something that anyone sensible should care about.

'Now, d'you think you can manage on the bar? And hold on to this at the same time.' He handed me the battered, old-fashioned gladstone bag in which – once I had seen it open in my mother's sickroom – he kept a jumble of medicine bottles, instruments and prescription pads. 'Fine.'

As we wobbled off into the slanting sunshine, with the trees casting shadows even longer than the one that he had cast in the garden, I could feel his presence, warm and smelling in no way disagreeably of sweat, enveloping me. His arms and legs from time to time brushed against my body, his breath was on my cheek. 'You can ring the bell, if you like. When there's some reason to ring it.' I at once rang it, although there was no reason.

Jack (that is what he told me to call him that day) lived in a small red-brick bungalow in the compound of the mission. It consisted of no more than a sitting room, a bedroom, a bathroom and a consulting room, outside the last of which, in the shady area beyond its french windows, groups of disconsolate Indians, patients and their families and even friends, would squat as they waited their summons. It was into the sitting room that he took me out of the heat and glare. 'No patients, not one. That's a marvel. I don't start to see them till five – except in an emergency. But they arrive at all hours. Sometimes I can't bear the sight of them, sitting impassive out there under the trees, and I start to see them earlier.'

Beyond the trees of which he spoke there was a small Victorian Gothic church, with a wooden spire that always seemed to me to lean slightly towards the bungalow. Beyond the bungalow, there was the substantial house, also of red brick, in which the Vellacotts lived.

I was gazing around me. I had never before visited the bungalow, although I had often visited the Vellacotts' house, both with my father and uncle and by myself, and although I had often, in the company of Clive, played in the straggly, overgrown garden in which house, bungalow and church all stood. A leather settee and two leather armchairs, all with bulbous arms over which hung strips of leather, weighted at either end, with ashtrays attached at the middle, stood pushed back against the walls, as though in preparation for a dance or a party. There was a single dirty sock on the settee and another on the floor beside it. In the middle of the room a rectangular kitchen table, the surface of its top scored and scratched, was covered with two wireless receivers, a separate loudspeaker, a battery, two transformers and a jumbled assortment of parts.

'Yep, that's it,' he said, following my gaze. 'Looks a mess, you don't have to tell me. But you'd be amazed what we can get.'

He sat down on the straightbacked ladder chair before the receiver and put out a hand to it. 'Take a pew.'

I pulled out a similar chair, the rush of its seat tattered as though a cat had been clawing at it, and watched and listened as he turned the knobs. There followed a cacophony of distant voices, snatches of music, atmospherics. Then, suddenly, we were both listening, intent.

'Do you know what that is?'

'Music,' I answered.

'Of course it's music, you chump.' He spoke with no ill nature. 'D'you know *what* music it is?'

My father and uncle, carefully stacking the records on top of one another on the record player and then glaring at me if I made the smallest movement or sound, would have known what music it was. I have never been musical, another disappointment for my father. I shook my head.

'Schubert. *Death and the Maiden*.' He put his head on one side and suddenly his face, with its freckles on high cheekbones — yes, now, almost fifty years later, it comes into focus for me — became pensive, even sad. For a while he went on listening, as though oblivious of my presence. Then he shook himself and once again began to twiddle with the knobs. 'D'you know where that music came from?'

'London?'

'No. Hilversum. D'you know where Hilversum is?' He laughed. 'Of course you don't! Hilversum's in Holland. I've never been there and you've never been there and yet here we are, in the middle of India, listening to a concert from Hilversum. That's what they call the wonder of science.'

The wonder of science. I think it was then, as the two of us sat facing each other, with the cumbrous receivers and the no less cumbrous loudspeaker and the jumble of parts between us, that I experienced, as though a hand had shoved an invisible boat out from the shore into a current that snatched at it, the first impetus towards the career in electronics that, to the dismay and bewilderment of my father, I was subsequently to follow.

For a little longer we listened to snatches of words and music from other parts of the world. Then Jack looked at his watch. 'Surgery in twenty minutes.'

I had never heard the word 'surgery' used in that sense before. 'Do you mean you have to do an operation on someone?'

[42]

He laughed loudly, showing his large, white teeth, one of which, in front, had a chip in it. 'Good God, no! I'm not a surgeon, though from time to time, yes, I do have to perform small operations. No, I mean I have to see my patients. My impatient patients,' he added. 'I'd better get you home.'

'I can find my own way.'

'Your uncle wouldn't be pleased if I let you do that.'

'Oh, I've often done it. When I used to visit Clive. Often, often.' That was a lie. I was never allowed out alone without at least an orderly.

'Sure?'

'Sure.' At that period, if I liked someone, I tended to speak in his or her way. Perhaps that was why my uncle did not care for me to play with Indian or Eurasian children. I now said that 'Sure' in Jack's drawling Canadian accent, not in my clipped English one.

Blinking at the sunlight, he came out with me into the garden. The impatient patients — though, sitting docilely under the trees, they looked extraordinarily patient to me — had already begun to arrive. One of them, a woman, her hand shielding her face with the edge of her sari, was rocking back and forth on her haunches, either in grief or in pain. Jack stared across at her. Then he said an odd thing, so out of character that I have remembered it, to puzzle over, during all the years since then. 'I hope she doesn't expect me to raise someone from the dead.'

. . . Suddenly, with a whisk of its tail and a flicker of its tongue, the lizard had vanished. Below my bedroom window, a man's voice, deep and jovial, had joined the women's. He must, I guessed, be teasing them, since each of his remarks was followed by piercing screams of laughter. Well, although it was only ten minutes to six, I was not going to sleep any more, that was certain. I got off the bed, my body stiff and aching, as it so often was after a long journey over Indian roads, shaved, showered, and dressed in shorts, open-necked shirt, cotton socks and gymshoes. When he had first seen me in this outfit, my father had looked me up and down and then said, 'You look like an overgrown schoolboy.' There was wonder, not malice, in his tone. 'I think he looks very natty,' Kirsti had defended me.

Before breakfast I should go for a walk, I decided. Having risen early to start on some journey, my father would sniff at the cool, damp air and then comment, 'The top of the morning.' I had never been wished 'The top of the morning' by anyone Irish. But I knew then, as I still know now, what the phrase, repeated over and over again by my father, meant at the start of a scorching Indian day. Briefly, there was the top of the morning, the rest was the dregs.

As I left my room, I all but stumbled over what seemed to be a bundle of rags outside my door. The bundle stirred, quickened into sudden life. Half shrouded by what I now saw to be a blanket, a grey face, the hair sticking up on end, revealed itself.

'Sahib! I am sorry, sahib! Very sorry, sahib!'

It was Rajiv, scrambling to his bare feet, the blanket held by one edge in nerveless fingers.

'What on earth are you doing here?'

All I felt was amazement, but clearly he mistook that amazement for anger, as he stammered out, 'Very sorry, sahib. I have slept too late. I will get car double quick.'

'Oh, we shan't be needing the car for two, three hours yet. But why are you sleeping here? Couldn't they find a room for you?'

He hung his head, as though in shame. 'Too much expense, sahib.'

'But my father told you we'd pay for it. Didn't you understand?'

'Yes, sahib. But too expensive. I am fine here. I am used to sleeping on floor.'

I shrugged, at once touched, exasperated and ashamed of what I had said the previous evening about his getting a rake-off from the hotel for having brought us to it. I walked on. There seemed nothing else to do.

. . . More than three weeks later, when we were about to say goodbye to Rajiv in Delhi and I was settling our account with him, I was again to feel at once touched, exasperated and ashamed in precisely the same manner.

I had held out a sheaf of banknotes. 'You'd better count them, in case I've made a mistake. It's the sum we agreed. And here' — I held out some more notes — 'is a little present. From all of us.'

Rajiv pushed the 'little present' into a pocket, without looking at it. Then, head bowed and brows drawn together, he began to pass the other tattered, scuffed notes, one by one, from one hand to the other, his lips silently counting as he did so. Eventually, he raised his head, his eyes squinting at me in what struck me as a curiously accusatory manner. 'Sahib, this is not right.'

Oh, Christ! Now we were going to have a lengthy argument, just when I was hot, tired and suffering from a headache after a day of sightseeing in a temperature several degrees above anything that we had so far known. 'Not right?' In my own ears my voice had a jagged edge to it. 'What do you mean — not right? That's precisely what we agreed, with the addition of what anyone would regard as a handsome tip.' My asking him to count the money had been merely a formality, I had not expected any dispute.

'Yes, sahib. Thank you, sahib. Tip very good, very nice. But you pay too much. Thirty-five rupees too much.'

'Too much!' I was stunned.

'I take you to Balram.'

'Yes, you took us to Balram. That's where we wanted you to take us. What about it?'

'But I take you too soon. I make mistake.'

'Oh, for heaven's sake!'

'Shorter distance. Many miles shorter.' He held out the money. 'Please, sahib.'

That I was determined not to take the notes had, I realize now, nothing to do with gratitude, generosity or affection – although at this moment, in the retrospect of so many years, I feel all those things for him. What impelled me was something less creditable, although even today I have difficulty in defining what precisely it was. Did I feel that he, an impoverished Indian, had no claim to the scruples of a rich (by his pitiful standards) Englishman like myself? Or did I resent an assertion of will by someone whom, in my arrogance, I felt to have no right to such a luxury?

'No, I don't want it. Certainly not!'

'Please, sahib!'

It seems to me now that, in continuing to thrust the notes at me, he was trying to tell me something about himself – or, at least, about his estimation of himself. But I was determined not to hear it. 'No, Rajiv! No!'

Kirsti and my father were walking across the yellowed lawn to join us, where we were holding our vehement parley in the evening shade of a clump of trees. That night Rajiv was

setting off on his long journey back to Udaipur – whether with or without passengers, he had been oddly reluctant to reveal, saying on one occasion 'Maybe' and on another 'I am not sure' when we had asked him.

At the sight of the others, he now stuffed the notes into the same pocket of his worn, dark blue cotton jacket into which he had already thrust the 'little present'.

Kirsti cried out, 'Oh, Rajiv, I feel so sad at saying goodbye to you. But we'll come back, next year or the year after that. And you'll drive us again, won't you?' Even then, I think that all of us – yes, Rajiv too – knew that nothing of the kind would ever happen.

Rajiv inclined his head slowly, until one could see nothing of his features, only the dark, crisp hair glistening with the oil that used to fill the car with its sickly perfume. Then he seemed to force himself to look up again, not at my father, much less at me, but at Kirsti. He drew a deep sigh.

I felt the need to bring these goodbyes to an end, as I should have felt the need to hurry people off a rickety bridge in imminent danger of collapse. I held out a hand. 'Goodbye, Rajiv. Thank you, thank you for everything.'

His hand was limp in mine, he did not look at me.

'Oh, Rajiv!' Impetuously, Kirsti put out her hands and grasped his forearms. I thought for a horrified moment that she was going to kiss him. But she merely looked into the face that he had now turned to her, its features no longer strained and taut but relaxing into a childlike wistfulness. 'How kind you've been, how kind. I'll never forget.' She gave him a little shake, then released him.

'Memsahib, I do not forget.' He said it as though it were a vow.

He now turned to my father. With grave formality, he brought the palms of his hands together before him and inclined not merely his head but his whole torso. He had often bowed like that to my father, but never to Kirsti or me.

Then, for the first time, solemnly, in no way making a joke of the salutation, my father brought his own hands together and bowed in return, his handsome, overlarge head making his body seem even more wispy than usual, as the head tipped forward and the thick white mane of hair — Kirsti and I had both been telling him that he must have it cut — tipped forward with it.

Without any further word, Rajiv turned abruptly away. His right hand went into the pocket into which he had thrust the money, he raised his left hand in the heavy air in a gesture of hesitant farewell. We watched in silence, as he hurried off across the grass without once looking back.

'Sad,' Kirsti said, when at last he had vanished. 'Oh, so sad.'

'*Ave atque vale*,' my father said. 'I wonder if we'll ever see him again.' He looked melancholy as he gazed out across the deserted, darkening lawn.

'Never,' I said, with cruel finality.

I all but told them of the argument over the money. Then I decided not to do so.

Late that evening, when we returned to the hotel from dinner, the clerk handed me a cheap-looking, crumpled, buff envelope along with my key. 'Your driver left this for you, sir.'

As I drew out the thirty-five rupees, with my father and Kirsti watching me, I knew that I now had to tell them of the argument. Heroically, Rajiv had persisted in making that assertion about himself which I had tried to balk him from making. For once, he had got the better of me.

We sat under a banyan tree, spreading in all directions around us, its bark like elephant hide, among the ruins of Shadibad. 'You know that "Shadibad" means "City of Joy", don't you?' my father had leant round in the car to say to Kirsti and me. We had, of course, known nothing of the kind. We were now eating the picnic lunch of processed cheese and ham between slices of soggy white bread, and hard-boiled eggs so small that they might have been laid by pigeons, which the hotel had provided.

Kirsti bit into a sandwich and began to chew on it. 'How wise Rajiv was to go off to get himself something from that stall. We should have done the same.'

My father ignored her, as he always ignored us if we had some grumble. He never cared about either food or comfort, and in any case his attitude to life's difficulties was always a stoical one of 'Bear them we can, And if we can, we must.' He began to attempt to peel a hard-boiled egg. But he was always maladroit at such simple operations and so, after he had spent some time picking at the cracked shell with the nail of a forefinger, Kirsti took it from him in her strong, capable hands.

As he watched her, my father began, 'Have you ever heard of anyone committing suicide by swallowing ground diamonds? A fine way to go, don't you think? Well, that's how Rupmati, the peasant girl wife of the last ruler, killed herself. Yes, captured by the Moguls, that's what she did. Swallowed ground diamonds, rather than become Akbar's concubine.' He spoke out of the melancholy that had seemed increasingly to envelop him during first our drive and then our wanderings about the ruins.

A dog had squatted some distance away from us, after having furtively circled us a number of times, his long tail and sharply pointed head both lowered, as though preparatory to cringing before an expected blow. Now he began to creep forward, almost on his belly, until I could make out the cruel lacerations, hair clotted round them, down one of his emaciated flanks. Perhaps he had been in a fight with some other of the dogs that we had seen roaming about the ruins, quick to scatter as we approached. Perhaps some human had inflicted the wounds. His huge, dark eyes, like the wounds themselves, were rimmed with flies, as though with pieces of jet.

'Poor creature,' Kirsti said. 'It's illogical and terrible, but I think the suffering of these animals has come to upset me more than the sufferings of the people.' She threw away what was left of the sandwich in her hand, as though she had no more appetite for it.

The dog, to whom she had not thrown it, began to slither forward inch by inch, as though in a macabre game of Grandmother's Footsteps. No doubt he was waiting for some shout, blow or stone, such as Rajiv, despite our protests, would administer if a pariah ever ventured near us. Then, suddenly valorous, the dog raced forward, grabbed the remains of the sandwich in his narrow jaws, and carried them off to the shade of a tree some distance from us.

My father now held out what was left of the sandwich from which he himself had just taken a fresh bite. 'Come, come, come! Don't be afraid! Come on, girlie!'

'Actually he's a boy,' I said.

He paid no attention to me. 'Come! Don't be afraid! We're not going to hurt you. Here! Here! Here!' Crouched forward on the rock on which he had perched, he seemed to be exerting all his will to make the pathetic, wary creature come to him. He extended the sandwich ever farther. 'Yes, yes, yes,' he crooned. Then he sighed out 'Yes' in quiet joy, since the dog was beginning to inch forward, his body so low on the ground that he was almost touching it. Miraculously, he all at once raised himself, wagged his tail and began to trot to my father.

As he chewed on the sandwich, shaking his head from side to side, the dog growled at the touch of my father's hand on his head and, fangs bared, seemed about to bite it. But once he had swallowed the sandwich with a gulp, he again wagged his tail. 'Pretty girl,' my father murmured, still caressing his head. 'Pretty' was hardly the adjective that I myself would have chosen. 'Pretty, pretty.' He raised his hand and held it out to the dog, palm upwards. The dog extended a long, red tongue and began to lick.

'That's not very wise,' Kirsti said.

'Why not?'

'Well . . . All the guidebooks say that one should beware of strays.'

'All the guidebooks are full of all kinds of nonsense.' He turned back to the dog. 'Yes, you're a beautiful girl, aren't you?'

I had difficulty in restraining myself from shouting out in exasperation, 'Boy, boy, boy!'

When we at last left our picnic site – Kirsti, with her usual Finnish scrupulousness, picked up even the fragments of eggshell, to place them in a paper bag – the dog for a long time trailed forlornly behind us, as though in the hope that we would adopt it. Then it dropped out of sight. With weary persistence, his melancholy seeming to have intensified even further, my father continued to lead us from ruined palace to ruined palace, even though, in the heat of the afternoon, there was scarcely another tourist in sight and Kirsti and I would much have preferred to lie out in the shade of a tree. All the time he lectured to us. Did we know that the fifteenth-century ruler Ghiasuddin had had fifteen thousand women in his harem? Now that was something, wasn't it? How on earth did we imagine that he had coped? At this spot — yes, it must have been here — there had been a parade of five hundred elephants to welcome the entry of another, later ruler, Jehangir. After a time, both Kirsti and I ceased to listen to him, apathetically trailing in his wake.

Then, as though a flame had begun to flicker in a wind, had diminished and had finally expired, my father fell silent. He trudged on, and we trudged on, now beside him and now behind him. His face had grown abstracted, he gazed up and around at things with no real interest. Kirsti caught my eye, looked over to him and then looked back at me, shrugging her shoulders and raising her eyebrows. Eventually I myself put the question that both gesture and look had implied. 'What's the matter, father?' Kirsti was by now some distance away from us, photographing a tamarind tree growing perilously close to where the ground plunged abruptly downwards for what seemed hundreds of feet.

'The matter? Nothing's the matter.' Before his recent marriage to Kirsti, I had from time to time seen him in this mood of abstraction, even distraction. I had then always assumed that he was thinking of my mother, so long irreplaceable until Kirsti, to everyone's astonishment, had replaced her.

'You seem — sad. Unlike your usual self.'

He gazed down at the ground, a hand stroking his chin. Then he looked up at me and smiled. 'You're sharp,' he said, though it had hardly needed sharpness to detect that all was not well. 'I awoke sad.'

'Why?'

[53]

'I awoke — don't ask me why — to this terrible sense of time going, going, gone. Do you remember those lines in the *Aeneid* — "*Nox ruit, Aenea*"?' Needless to say, I didn't, and it was perhaps because he knew that I didn't that he now translated for me: '"Night is rushing down, Aeneas." That's what I feel, old chap. It's as though one were gardening and there were so many things still to do — plants to be bedded out, grass to be cut, roses to be pruned — and then, all at once, long before one had expected, the dusk is beginning to fall, so quick, oh so quick. There's so much I still have to do, and so little time left in which to do it.'

For me there was a terrible pathos in this confession. Having inherited a modest fortune from my mother, he could, had he only had the will and the perseverance, have brought to completion at least some of the projects on which in his youth he had set forth with so much ardour, only to let them slip gradually, year by year, from nerveless fingers. For almost as long as I could remember he had been tinkering with a book about architecture, of which I knew nothing but its title, once glimpsed on a folder left lying, perhaps deliberately so that I should see it, on the sitting-room table. *Frozen Music*. I'd liked the title — taken (it was Kirsti who eventually told me this) from a phrase of Ruskin's about Venice. I also knew that, during his years of vagabondage in India, he had been working on another book about — he was never more explicit — 'the social life of the Raj'. There had been yet other books planned, discussed with friends, even begun as notes jotted down in lined school exercise books. But what he had actually published had been pathetically meagre: an introduction to an extravagantly priced book of photographs of European architecture in India, put out by his own firm; a few articles on paintings of the Deccani school; and some translations of

Catullus and Horace, printed years before in an anthology, which I had never read. In short, almost every task in the garden was still to be completed; and if, as he now told me, he felt the imminence of night, then uncompleted they would remain.

There was, therefore, a cruel irony in his confession of the reason for his sadness on that day in Shadibad. But there is now an even crueller irony in his survival, a frail, deaf octogenarian, obstinately refusing to leave his house for a home — 'A home is not a home,' he has wryly remarked to me more than once — even to the moment when I sit writing this while, out in our garden, our guest now till his death, he jots down more notes in yet another lined school exercise book for some further project doomed never to be realized.

Kirsti walked towards us, camera in hand. Then she raised it quickly and clicked. 'Got you!' she cried out, as though she had bagged two tigers in the jungle. Behind her, there was Rajiv, back from his meal and, no doubt, one of those siestas in which he would lie sprawled out in the shade of some tree or building as though he were dead. He put his hand up to shield his eyes, a familiar gesture, and then gazed not at my father, not at me and not at the ruins around us but at Kirsti. 'Beautiful,' he said. He seemed to be saying it not about Shadibad but about her.

On our return journey, in contrast to my father, who remained slumped in gloom, Rajiv was euphoric. As a rule, he did not speak except either to point out something that he thought we had missed or to answer a question. But now, unprompted by anything other than the sight of three ragged, bare-footed, motionless children standing, as though lost, at the place, shaded by tall trees, where the road from Shadibad joined the main thoroughfare, he began to speak of his family in a high-pitched, excited voice, from time to time turning his head — sometimes even in the face of oncoming traffic — to address Kirsti and me in the back of the car. 'I am often thinking of my children. Today, I say to myself, "What are the baba doing now?" I do not know. Maybe they are enjoying, maybe they are flying kites or playing with chums. But maybe one is sick, maybe both are sick. I am worried.' But despite this last confession, his tone was oddly buoyant. How terrible, I thought, to live in a world in which no communication with absent loved ones was possible by picking up a telephone. 'I am happy with my children, boy and girl, but children are also worry. That is truth. Luckily my wife is good, much better than I. She is educated lady, daughter of bank employee. Before marriage, she was schoolteacher. Maybe, when children are older, she will be schoolteacher again. I do not wish it, mother's place is in the home, but she wishes it. Teaching is important for her.'

As he rattled on, so unusually communicative and jolly, I wondered whether he might not be high on something. It could not be alcohol, since he had so often refused the beer that we had offered to him, telling us that he never drank. But might it not be the *ganja* about which he had once told us, after Kirsti, noticing some plants of it growing in a field, had asked what it was? He and his friends or he and his family, he said, would often smoke it convivially after the day's work was over. It was cheap, he could get some for us, if we wished to try it. 'No problem,' he added, using a phrase learned from the many Americans whom he had driven. We guessed that he must frequently have obtained *ganja* for his Western passengers.

Eventually he fell silent, probably for lack of encouragement from my father, long since asleep, or from Kirsti and me, who were almost so. Now, instead of talking, he began a soft, toneless whistle, almost a hissing, like a kettle on the boil.

When at last we drew up in front of the hotel — the journey back, as so often, had seemed much longer than the journey out — he jumped out of the car with alacrity, rushed round to pull open the door beside Kirsti, and then — something he had never done before for her — put out a hand to help her out. She smiled up at him, not wholly concealing her surprise. 'Thank you.'

'Thank *you*, lady.' It struck me as an odd response.

Hands pressed to the small of his back, my father stretched himself. 'Ah, I'm tired.' It was the first time that he had ever admitted to tiredness on our journey, though Kirsti and I often did so. And, yes, he did look tired, his face grey and his eyelids puffy. He put a hand to his throat, stroking it gently and then pressing on one side. 'I seem to have a sore patch — just here.' Again he pressed. Then he gave a grimace.

'Why has he gone to bed so early?'

On the yellowish-brown patch of grass before the hotel, someone had set out tables and chairs. Kirsti and I sat, dinner over, at the table that seemed to have been least spattered by birds, waiting for the beers that we had asked the indolent, handsome waiter in the restaurant to bring out to us.

'I don't know.' Kirsti had that anxious look, as of a mother for an ailing child, that I had come to know so well and that somehow always irritated me. My father was twice her age and yet it might have been the other way about. 'He tired himself today. He has this sore throat, although, when I looked into it, I could see nothing but a slight redness. And he seems, well, despondent. Don't ask me why.'

[57]

'Perhaps he's worrying about our visit to Balram.'

'Perhaps. So many memories, terrible memories, sad memories. Not easy.' She tilted back her head to gaze up at the immense sweep of starry sky above us. 'Perhaps it would be easier if I were not with you.'

'Nonsense.' But I thought that she might well be right.

'It's not easy for me either,' she said.

'I can see that.'

'Or for you,' she added.

'Oh, I don't know.'

'You must have loved your mother. And to lose her at that age . . . Traumatic, yes?'

I thought for a while. 'Perhaps that's why I've never been much good with women. Until I went to university I knew so few.'

'Did you and your father often talk about your mother?'

'Very seldom. Hardly at all. That's what's odd. He only began to talk about her when you came along.' Should I have revealed that? Looking across at her, I was not sure. 'It was as though his love for you somehow awakened a remembrance of that other love.'

'That figures.'

I wanted to pursue the conversation, and yet I was frightened of where, by winding paths and over hidden obstacles, it might eventually take us, as we sat alone together in this new intimacy, by a main road once so busy and now almost totally bare of traffic. I glanced over my shoulder. 'What's happened to that beer?'

'You're not so optimistic as to suppose it'll ever come, are you?'

'Shall I go in and remind them?'

'No, no, don't do that.' I felt a sharp pang of disappointment as she picked her bag up off the table and slowly rose. 'I think I'd better go in to him. See if he's all right.'

'I wonder what he's got planned for us tomorrow.'

'Hasn't he told you?'

'Not yet. I meant to ask him at dinner and then I forgot.'

'Horrible dinner. But, as always, the poor dear didn't notice. That's sometimes rather discouraging at home, you know. I go to enormous trouble to prepare him something out of Elizabeth David and, for all he cares, it might as well be baked beans on toast.' She moved away from the table, then raised her handbag in a valedictory gesture. 'Goodnight, Rupert. Don't sit here too long or you'll be bitten to death by these gnats.'

'Goodnight, Kirsti.'

I watched as, erect and sure-footed, she descended the sloping lawn and then began to crunch across the gravel to the entrance of the hotel. I felt moved, as so often in the past, by her air of health and sturdiness. I could well understand why, when she had been nursing my father in St Thomas's after his prostate operation, he had fallen in love with her. What I found less easy to understand was why she had fallen in love with him. 'Poor Philip', 'poor dear', 'poor darling': perhaps in that constant 'poor' there lay the clue. She had to give out of the emotional riches of her life to the emotional poverty of his, just as my father had to give out of his financial riches to the financial poverty of the Indians.

Feet again crunched on the gravel, disturbing my reverie. It was the indolent, handsome waiter, with the long, dirty fingernails and turban rakishly askew. He was carrying a tin tray, with two glasses, their interiors beaded with drops of water, and two bottles of beer.

'Where is your wife, sahib?' he asked.

I should have corrected him, but did not do so. 'She got tired of waiting and went up to bed.'

'Very busy tonight, sahib. I run here, I run there.' I did not believe him. When we had eaten dinner, the restaurant had been empty but for two elderly American women, who sat with an array of pill bottles set out before them, as though the pills, of various sizes and colours, were part of their meal. 'I am sorry, sahib. Both bottles open now.' He had already set down the tray. Now he raised his hands, the palms pink, in an expressive gesture.

'Never mind.' I signed the chit, then brought some small change out of my trouser pocket for a tip. 'I'll drink both.'

'I put on light for you, sahib?' He indicated what looked like a rusty metal funnel stuck into the ground, with an aperture, inset with a light, at its top.

I shook my head. 'No, that's all right, thank you. The light'll attract even more insects.'

I sipped at the beer, which, unlike most beer served in India, was lukewarm. Staring up into the wide, starry sky, as Kirsti had done before me, I began to think of her entering that suite described by my father as looking as if it had belonged to an oriental Miss Havisham. Was my father asleep under that frayed, dusty silk canopy? Slumped gloomily in one or other of the sagging leather chairs? Fretfully turning over the pages of some guidebook as he made notes for tomorrow's itinerary? I saw her standing behind him, her hand resting lightly on the back of his neck. I saw her tiptoeing past the bed in which he snored, as she made her way to the bathroom. I saw his arms, the veins like purple cords, going out to embrace her as she slipped into the bed beside him.

I had never been close to him and now, after all these days, a seemingly endless string of them, in which I had been constantly in his company as I had never been during all those years when we had lived together in the same house, I was still no closer. I wished then, as I wish even now, that I had done something in my life in which he could take pride: won a scholarship to Oxford instead of merely scraping in; achieved an effortless First, instead of a hard-won Second; written a novel or a symphony; married a wife who was his intellectual equal or superior, instead of being merely rich; fathered precocious children, candidates for Mensa.

Suddenly, unbidden, as though bile, bitter and caustic, had jetted up in my throat, a memory came back to me. It was the summer regatta at the public school to which he had sent me because it had been his own, and for once — usually he forgot or ignored Speech Days and Parents' Days — he had come on a visit. I was to compete in the Diamond Sculls.

'The Diamond Sculls, the Diamond Sculls? What are they?' he had asked me, as though I were about to compete in a game of Ludo or Tiddlywinks. Surely, as an old boy, he must know about the Diamond Sculls?

Eventually I had had to leave him to go down to the boathouse to get myself ready.

'You'll be able to look after yourself, won't you?'

He had laughed. 'Of course! You seem to forget that I was at this place myself. What I'll do is toddle along to the library for a chat with old Newcombe and then I'll come on down to the river in time for the race.'

'You know where to go?'

'I didn't row myself. But of course I know. Don't be an ass!'

That was the year when I won the Diamond Sculls. But my father did not see me win.

'Oh dear, I was late, I'm afraid. I walked over to the library, as I said I'd so, and then, well, I lost all account of time. Old

Newcombe has recently acquired this holograph of a Philip Sidney poem, you must have seen it, I imagine.' Needless to say, I did not even know of its existence. 'A snip. Bought privately from some estate. No one knew it even existed. Fascinating!'

Years later I had had a similar experience with the first girl with whom I had ever fallen in love. She was giving a birthday party in her room in Somerville and, since she had let fall that she needed a new toaster, I had bought her the most expensive I could find.

'Oh, Rupert, how *angelic* of you!' she had exclaimed, taking the carefully wrapped parcel from me while also looking out, frowningly, over my shoulder to see who next would come.

Then some more guests had shoved their way into the tiny room, and she had thrown down the present, unopened, among the coats, hats and umbrellas strewing her bed.

When we next met, she had never even referred to the toaster. I had bought it at a time when I had been exceptionally short of money.

But the pain of that first disappointment inflicted by my father had been far more acute and lasting than the pain of this second inflicted by a girl whose features, oddly, I cannot now reassemble in my memory, even though I can still see every detail of her room.

. . . Presents. As I write this, I all at once remember not merely that humiliation over a present, but another, later one.

When I had proposed to Caroline, then working in the jewellery department of one of the leading fine-art auctioneers, it was in the honest belief that she was as hard up as myself. Her father, she had told me, had some kind of construction business in one of the Gulf states, and from that I had naively imagined him to be some superior kind of builder.

Then, shortly before the wedding, I met him. He and Caroline's mother, who had been on the stage, were staying at Claridge's in a suite full of waxen flowers in huge urns. I remarked, insincerely, on their beauty. 'Our Arab friends are always so generous,' Caroline's mother said in a self-satisfied tone, crossing her feet at the ankles and then placing one small hand on top of the other on her lap. 'They can afford to be,' Caroline retorted, with that sharpness that she had not yet come to show to me.

Her Glasgow-born father had a large, square head, with the blond hair cut so short that one could see the scalp through it. If there is one adjective that now recalls him for me, it is 'loud'. His deep, nasal voice was loud, the checks of his suits were loud, and there was a loudness about the frankness and vehemence of his opinions and the unsubtlety, even brutality, of the questions that he discharged at me. In the Jaguar that he had hired, the blare of the radio — whether relaying pop music or the news, it never seemed to be off — made it necessary to shout to carry on any kind of conversation. 'Couldn't you turn that down, darling?' his pretty, brittle wife would beg him, and Caroline would add, 'Or, better still, turn it right off?' But he never listened to either of them.

He was a kind, generous man, and he adored Caroline, his only child. 'Why she took that job, I just don't understand,' he told me. 'For God's sake, she doesn't *need* to work. She could have come out to us and had a good time.' Perhaps he was thinking that, if she had done that, she would not have become engaged to someone as dim and wet as me.

Soon after our marriage, when Caroline had moved from the flat she had been sharing with a girl colleague in Royal Avenue into my flat in Albert Bridge Road, she began to ask me about my dead mother. 'So she had the cash,' she said. Like her father, she was interested in money, even if, unlike him, she was not interested in making it or even spending it. I nodded. She laughed. 'Then it runs in the family!' 'What runs in the family?' Still not used to her cruelty, I genuinely did not know what she was getting at. 'Marrying rich women,' she said.

That was a time when, although I found it easy to be hurt, I did not find it easy to say hurtful things. I made no answer.

I had no idea what financial arrangements existed between Caroline and her father. She never told me, I never asked. From time to time, she would suddenly propose what to me, with my tiny salary, seemed an extravagance – a weekend in Paris, expensive tickets to hear Joan Sutherland at Covent Garden, new curtains from Harvey Nichols for the sitting-room windows. Then when I protested, she would reply, 'Oh, don't work yourself into a tizzy! I'm not asking *you* to pay. Daddy's sent a cheque.'

It is difficult to love someone to whom one cannot be generous. I wanted so much to be generous to her. That was how, every two or three weeks when I had some money to spare, I came to buy her piece after piece of the Rosenthal dinner service. We had first seen it in Fortnum's when we had gone in there for a snack after a visit to an exhibition at Burlington House. 'Oh, isn't that the most beautiful thing you ever saw?' I had seen many more beautiful things, there were even more beautiful Rosenthal dinner services in Fortnum's that day. But I said that, yes, it was certainly beautiful. She ran a forefinger round the rim of a plate that seemed to me altogether too shiny and smooth. 'So pure, so simple, so strong.'

I would come home from work and 'I have something for you!' I would call out, breathless as much from what was almost a sexual excitement as from a climb up eighty-seven stairs.

'Another piece! Oh, darling, you *are* good to me.'

'When we have the whole set, twelve of everything, we're going to give a dinner party.'

'For twelve people?'

'Of course.'

'In this flat? Darling, you're bonkers. If you want a dinner party for twelve, then we'll have to find somewhere else to live.'

That was the winter when, for weeks on end, I suffered from what our doctor, an elderly woman, eventually diagnosed as 'a low-grade virus', since she could produce no other diagnosis. When I was not shivering, I was sweating. The eighty-seven stairs suddenly seemed to be eight hundred and seven. When Caroline said that this or that friend of hers — I had few friends myself and none in whom Caroline ever showed any interest — had asked us to a party, I'd tend to say, 'You go, darling, I honestly still don't feel up to it. Oh, I do wish I could throw off this thing!'

One night she returned from one such party, given by the editor of one of those free magazines full of articles about expensive restaurants and holidays, and advertisements for expensive cars and houses. Her eyes were unusually bright, her speech slightly slurred. She stood, swaying slightly in the doorway of our bedroom, in the silver-fox coat that her father had given her for Christmas. (I remember how shocked and distressed my own father had been, when she had proudly told him that, no, the fur wasn't simulated, it was real.)

'In bed already!' She laughed. 'Well, I suppose that's convenient!' She slipped off the fur coat, dropped it on the floor, and approached the bed.

For a time all had gone well. Then I had felt an extraordinary weakness, not merely of the muscles, not merely of the bones, but even of the marrow within the bones. The sweat had begun to prick through my forehead, I could feel it trickling down my breastbone, as though it were some insect making its way by exploratory fits and starts.

'Sorry, sorry, sorry . . . I don't know what's the matter with me. I suppose it's this wretched bug.'

She heaved herself up from under me. Her eyes were shining even more brightly than before, her cheeks were flushed. She looked extraordinarily beautiful. She left me wholly unmoved.

She clambered off the bed, she knelt beside it. 'I'm going to make you come, if it's the last thing I do – or the last thing you do.'

I remember thinking that it was a curious kind of fastidiousness that she should do what she was doing and yet never once touch me with her hands. The hands lay on the eiderdown, on either side of my thighs.

'Oh, for Christ's sake!' Eventually, she had to give up.

Shivering in the bathroom, I stared at my pallid reflection in the mirror, a thermometer in my mouth. 'A hundred and one,' I called out to her. It was my alibi, my excuse. But, lying in the bed, her face turned towards the wall and her knees drawn up, she did not answer.

When I came home from work the following day – she started and finished work earlier than I – she summoned me from the sitting room which also served as a dining room, 'Surprise for you, darling! Lovely surprise!' That morning she

[66]

had been morose, surly. When I had tried to kiss her, she had turned her head away. Now her voice was buoyant, even joyful.

Still in my overcoat, I hurried into the sitting room.

'Look!'

I looked. On the dining table, completely covering it, the whole resplendent Rosenthal dinner service lay stacked. 'Isn't that terrific?' she said. 'Now all we've got to do is find that bigger flat — and count whether we have as many as twelve friends to invite to dinner to celebrate.'

I stared at the dinner service. As I felt the tears gathering in my eyes, I tried to persuade myself that they were merely the result of the cold wind out on Albert Bridge on my walk home across it.

'There was this cheque from Daddy,' she said. 'So I rang up Fortnum's. I ordered the lot.'

What were my father and Kirsti doing now? Perhaps they lay locked, motionless, in each other's arms? Perhaps he slept, mouth open while he snored, and she still sat up, bare legs outstretched before her on the sofa, a book in her lap? Perhaps they were even now making love? *Did* they make love? Yes, surely they must. But I hated to think of that. With a conscious exertion of the will, I tried to erase the picture.

I drained my glass of beer and left Kirsti's undrunk. I got up, suddenly feeling achy and tired, and began slowly to go in.

THREE

BY THE TIME, two days later, that we set off on the drive back to Balram, my father had lost his voice. There were hectic spots on his cheekbones, emphasized by the greyness of the skin around them and by the dullness of the eyes above. He moved with an effortful weariness.

'He absolutely refuses to have his temperature taken,' Kirsti told me in a low voice, as my father was whispering his thanks to the various servants standing around the car, no doubt in the expectation of yet again being tipped, and even, to their amazement, shaking them by their hands. 'Why does he have to be so obstinate?'

'Always has been. You must have realized that by now.'

My father rejoined us. Taking me by an arm, he croaked hoarsely, 'Give them something each. They've all been so kind and helpful.'

I felt ashamed that I could not share in his opinion of their kindness and helpfulness. 'Oh, all right!' I put a hand into my back trouser pocket and pulled out some notes. The servants crowded round me, like scattered filings to a magnet.

In the car, I said, 'I wish you'd let Kirsti take your temperature, father.'

'I haven't got a temperature,' he answered fretfully.

'How can you possibly know that,' Kirsti put in, 'if you don't let me take it?'

'One always knows if one has a temperature. I know that I haven't. This kind of throat is common in India. Often used to have it in the old days. The dust, that's what causes it. Don't you remember that Australian couple we met in Udaipur?'

Sitting next to us at dinner, there had been these two extraordinarily handsome people, each with the physique of an athlete. Anyone would have been struck by them anywhere. They had smiled up at us as we had taken our places. But we noticed that, whenever they had anything to say to each other — which was not often — they put their heads close, as though to ensure that we did not overhear them. In the middle of the meal, the girl suddenly threw down her napkin on the table and hurried out of the room. The man first stared gloomily at her vacant place and then leant over to me — I was closest to him — to whisper hoarsely, 'I'm afraid my wife's succumbed to the trots. And I've picked up this laryngitis. What a way to spend a honeymoon!'

'Of course I remember them,' Kirsti now said. 'And you ought to remember that they told us that they were on antibiotics.'

'The body has its own defences against this kind of thing.'

'Anyway, suck one of these,' Kirsti said, opening her bag and producing some cough lozenges.

'They taste foul,' my father complained with the petulance of a child.

'Suck it!'

Even in his present condition, my father could not restrain himself from turning round to us whenever we passed anything of note. 'That's an interesting *torna* over there. . . .

Yes, that must be the town where, improbably, there's said to be a fine museum. . . . Oh, yes, yes, I remember that stupa. What's so interesting about it . . .' From time to time he would suggest that we should stop in order to look at something either remembered from the past or read about in the present. But Kirsti, surprising me by her firmness, would have none of that. Wandering around in the heat, she said, was the worst possible thing for him; we'd better push on; the sooner we reached Balram, the better.

Once again we forced our way, by abrupt jerks forward and no less abrupt halts, through streets jammed with cars, carts, bicycles, pedestrians, indifferently straying cattle and stray dogs. Rajiv kept his thumb constantly on the horn, as did every other driver. My father put his hands to his ears. 'This din! How can they bear to live all their lives in this constant din?' It was the first time that he had ever complained about it, though Kirsti and I had often done so.

'Sorry, sahib. If I do not hoot, then maybe I will kill some person.'

'Yes, of course, of course,' my father croaked.

Rajiv, whose first visit to Balram had been when he had driven us through it three days before and who therefore had no idea of the whereabouts of the Akbar Inn Hotel, kept repeating 'It is in Dalhousie Square, Dalhousie Square,' as he consulted the map open on his knees, while at the same time continuing to edge the car through the traffic.

'But where *is* Dalhousie Square?' I demanded impatiently.

'Here on map, sahib.'

'And where are *we* on the map?'

To that it was clear that poor Rajiv did not know the answer.

Kirsti put a hand on his shoulder. 'Ask someone, Rajiv.'

Had I made that suggestion, Rajiv might have ignored it, as so often in the past. But now he said docilely, 'Yes, memsahib, I will ask.' He put his head out of the open window beside him and shouted to an emaciated old man, each bone of his rib-cage distinct, who was pushing a handcart alongside us. The man stopped and we ourselves stopped, with the result that all the cars behind us began to hoot even more frantically. The old man shook his head and asked a younger man carrying two scrawny chickens, still alive, upside down by their legs. This man also shook his head and turned to a ragged boy. Soon a crowd had collected, among them a plump, prosperous-looking, copiously sweating man in a grey pinstripe suit and canary yellow panama hat, a furled umbrella over an arm. It was he who finally told us the route, drawing on the dust on the roof of the car, with Rajiv standing attentive beside him. The owner of the Akbar Inn Hotel was, he told us, a cousin of his. The hotel was first class, A1.

From that sign glimpsed by the roadside on our first journey through Balram, I had in my mind an image of a square, porticoed building with a semicircular drive sweeping up and away from it. I was therefore amazed when Rajiv swung the car towards what appeared to be a garage. Near-naked mechanics, their scant clothing and bodies smeared with grease, were lying under dented chassis, crawling over engines, changing tyres, hammering, washing, polishing.

'This can't possibly be it.'

'Yes, sahib. Akbar Inn Hotel. Best hotel in Balram.'

Rajiv craned out of the window beside him, tilting back his head, and pointed upwards. I similarly craned out of the window beside me. High up, on the roof of the building, there was a crooked wooden board: 'Akbar Inn Hotel'.

'Well, yes, this does seem to be it.' I opened my door.

The entrance was round the corner. A beggar was propped up in front of it, a shrivelled leg stuck out and a crutch, its support bound round with rags, resting beside him. He extended a cupped hand, while at the same time crooning, 'Baksheesh, baksheesh!' Kirsti and I walked past, into the cool of the entrance hall, but my father dithered for a while outside, muttering hoarsely, 'Oh, I don't know . . . I don't seem to have . . . Oh, Rupert . . . Oh, I give up . . .' as he fumbled in his pockets.

Kirsti called out over her shoulder, as she began to mount the concrete steps in front of us, 'Later, Philip! You can give him something later.'

Rajiv, pushing past my still dithering father, shouted up the stairwell. Almost at once there was a babble of voices above us, followed by the clatter of three boys racing down. They halted briefly as they came face to face with Kirsti and me on the stairs, then, chanting out almost in unison, 'Sorry, sorry sorry!' they hurtled past us to fetch our luggage.

Well, at least the lobby looked clean, I took in three rattan chairs, on one of which a scholarly-looking Indian sat reading an English-language newspaper, a rattan table covered with ancient magazines and paperbacks, no doubt left there by previous travellers, and an elaborately carved wooden hatstand.

A huge man, the ends of his black moustache reaching to his round dimpled chin, lumbered to his feet from the diminutive armchair into which he had somehow squeezed himself behind the reception desk. His complexion was pale enough to pass for European. He was wearing a massive signet ring, engraved, I was surprised to see, with a Star of David.

Beginning with my father and then going on to me and finally to Kirsti, he shook each of us by the hand. Having done that, he clasped his plump hands before him and gave a little bow. 'We are honoured to have you here as our guests. You had a good journey?'

Kirsti was the one who answered, 'Yes, thank you, except that we had difficulty in locating the hotel.'

'Difficulty?' He seemed unable to credit it.

At that moment the three boys arrived panting up the stairs with our luggage, followed by Rajiv, who was empty-handed. Turning, Rajiv gave them some imperious directions in Hindi, pointing to a corner of the lobby in which he clearly wished them to make a stack. Quickly they complied.

'Our driver doesn't come from these parts,' Kirsti told the manager. Then she smiled across at Rajiv, who smiled back. 'In fact he comes from hundreds and hundreds of miles away. So he'd no idea of the way.'

'What also complicated things was that I'd seen an advertisement of yours as one drives in from the west,' I added. 'It had led me to expect something – different.'

'Different?' The manager looked vaguely affronted.

I hesitated whether to explain the discrepancy between the building depicted on the poster and the one in which we had found ourselves, but decided that it was really too much bother. 'Anyway, here we are,' I said instead.

'Yes, here you are,' the manager confirmed. 'Please let me introduce myself. I am manager of this hotel, and my name is Mr Solomon.'

Even as he spoke the name, I heard in my mind something like the faint echo of a bell tolling far off in the distance.

'Mr Solomon?'

'That is correct, sir.'

The echo grew louder, sharpened in definition.

'Did you have a relative who worked on the railway?'

He stared at me, mouth loosely open to reveal that two of his bottom front teeth had been capped with gold. Clearly he had decided that I was gifted with extraordinary powers of ESP. 'Yes, sir, indeed, sir. My dad — who is no longer in the land of the living, I regret — worked for the railway.'

'I thought so! I remember now. He was my uncle's assistant. Yes! Do you remember, father?'

But my father, who had sunk into the rattan chair opposite the one occupied by the scholarly-looking man with the newspaper, clearly remembered nothing. 'What?' he croaked. 'Remember what?'

My Uncle Claud bullied Mr Solomon. Even now I could hear his voice: 'Oh, for God's sake, man!' Or: 'Oh, don't be such a blithering idiot!' Or: 'Get a move on!' Mr Solomon, always smiling sweetly and always eager to carry out any order, seemed not to mind; and that he seemed not to mind puzzled me then as it continues to puzzle me now. 'Yes, sir, yes, sir, very good, sir,' he would rattle off automatically, as he went about a task. Unlike his son, he was small and compact, with a hooked nose, thin lips and a purple birthmark, the size of a 10p piece, on one of his temples. He used to call me 'Laddie' when addressing me, and 'the little man' when referring to me. He was (so my uncle had told me) the son of a white businessman and a woman from Kashmir.

'My uncle was managing director of the railway. Your father was his chief assistant.'

'Mr Reynolds?' Mr Solomon spoke the name with a notable lack of enthusiasm.

I nodded. 'My father and I stayed with him here in Balram.'

[74]

I almost added, 'My mother died here,' then something restrained me.

Mr Solomon waddled behind the desk. 'May I please ask you to register, sir?' Clearly he had no wish to pursue the conversation.

My father remained seated, his head bowed and a hand to his forehead, as Kirsti and I filled in our particulars.

'You will wish to know the charges,' Mr Solomon said when we had finished. Before we could reply, he began to rattle them off.

'That seems very reasonable,' Kirsti said — as, indeed, they were.

'I must ask you to switch off the light when not in the rooms. Likewise the air-conditioning. In India electricity is very dear.'

'We'll do that,' I said.

He handed a cumbrous key to Kirsti and a similar one to me. He smiled. 'These keys are difficult to lose or take away with one in one's pocket.' He waddled out from behind the desk. 'Permit me. I will show you the way.' His voice suddenly acquiring a peremptory edge, he shouted out in Hindi to the three boys, who were standing, legs apart and hands behind their backs, before our pile of luggage, as though to guard it. At once they began hurriedly to pick it up.

'Come along, Philip.'

As my father slowly rose, staggered a little, and then took a faltering step towards us, the Indian in the other chair stared at him over the top of his newspaper with blatant curiosity. Kirsti scanned my father's face and then frowned at what she found there. 'How are you, darling?'

My father put out his arms as though he were about to embrace her. His mouth opened. Then he jerked up from within him what was more a retch than a groan, turned his head sideways, his eyelids fluttering wildly, and collapsed on the floor.

The three boys retreated in terror. Rajiv let out an inarticulate cry. Mr Solomon, plump hands raised to his cheeks, exclaimed, 'Oh, my goodness!'

Kirsti, admirably calm, knelt down on the ground beside my father, fingers at once going to the pulse at his wrist. I stood over her. She looked up. 'Help me. Let's lift him up into the chair.' Already my father's eyes were once again fluttering. Then they opened wide, with an initial look of terror in them.

'Some water,' Kirsti said to Mr Solomon.

The Indian in the chair now rose to his feet, the newspaper still held in both his hands. He stared down at my father with a look of fastidious distaste. Then he began to edge away towards the reception desk.

Mr Solomon shouted at one of the boys, who rushed off. Rajiv crept nearer. Then, as Kirsti and I began to lift my father, he stooped to join in. 'Is sahib dying?' he turned to me to ask as we heaved.

'Of course not, you fool!' But at that moment the terrible fear had come to me that he might indeed be dying.

Slowly my father revived. Kirsti held the glass of water, its rim smeared as though someone had already drunk from it, up to his lips, and, like a bird, he then took small swallows, tilting his head back yet farther.

'It is the heat,' the previously silent Indian with the newspaper now came over to tell us. 'Dehydration.'

'But it's not hot here,' Kirsti said. 'It's air-conditioned.'

'You have been travelling in the heat of the day,' the Indian explained with weary patience, as though to a halfwit.

Eventually, with Kirsti and me supporting him on either

side, my father managed to walk to their room. Like the lobby, it was clean, with the same floor of marble chips and the same rattan furniture. 'Lie down,' Kirsti told him, as Mr Solomon, Rajiv and the three boys peered in through the open door. Docilely, he obeyed her, giving a little groan, a feeble echo of the terrifying earlier one, as he lowered himself on to the nearest of the two beds and then drew up first one leg and then the other. Kirsti stooped and, with an extraordinary gentleness and concern, began to remove his shoes.

Mr Solomon now crossed the threshold. 'I will adjust the air-conditioning,' he announced, as though he had just reached a momentous decision. He drew a key from his pocket, went over to the air-conditioning unit and unlocked its padlock.

'It's all right, all right,' my father croaked, once again unwilling that anyone should give him special treatment. But Mr Solomon made the adjustment. As he did so, I wondered – unworthily, as it later transpired – if he would make a compensating adjustment to our bill.

'Thank you. You've been very kind. I think what he needs now is some rest.' Kirsti crossed over to the door.

Reluctantly Mr Solomon followed her. He turned to me. 'Do you wish to see your room now?'

'Later. For the moment I'll stay here with my father. Perhaps the boys would take my luggage along?' I held out the key.

'Certainly, sir. Come to me at the desk when you are ready, if you will be so good.'

As Mr Solomon waddled off down the corridor, followed by the still awestruck boys – I realized, as they disappeared, that I had forgotten to tip them – Rajiv put his head round the by now half-shut door. 'Is sahib all right?'

His concern was so clearly genuine that I felt guilty for having shouted at him over my father's prostrate body in the lobby. 'Yes, I think so. We won't need the car again today. Go and have a rest. And, please, this time be sure to get yourself a room at our expense. No more sleeping on the floor!'

As though he had not heard me, he said, 'I will wait for you in lobby, sahib.'

Trying to keep the exasperation out of my voice, I told him, 'It's not necessary, Rajiv. Have a rest.'

'I will wait,' he replied, as he went off down the corridor.

Kirsti was seated on the edge of the bed beside my father, whose eyes were now shut. She held his hand in hers, as though in an effort to transmit to him her own health and robustness. 'You've got to see a doctor,' she said. 'Did you hear me, Philip? You've got to see a doctor.'

'Not necessary.'

'Yes. Look at you. You're shivering. You must have a fever.' She relinquished his hand and rose from the bed. 'In fact, I'm going to get that Mr — Mr Solomon to get you a doctor now. At once.'

'No, Kirsti.'

'Yes! Don't argue.'

He tossed his head fretfully from side to side, as both of us looked down at him. Then he said, 'Oh, very well, very well.' Suddenly he opened his eyes wide and stared up at the ceiling. 'There used to be this doctor. A Canadian. What was his name?' It was odd that, at that moment, neither he nor I could recall Jack Mackenzie's name. 'Good doctor, good man. Looked after Irene, you know. But I don't suppose he's still here. Probably went back home a long time ago.'

'Well, I'll ask Mr Solomon. He'll know who to call.' She looked over to me. 'Keep an eye on him till I get back.'

'Of course. Unless you'd like me to ask Solomon.'

'No. You stay here.'

After she had gone, my father raised himself on an elbow. 'Poor old Kirsti! I'm afraid my little turn must have given her a shock.'

'It gave me a shock too.'

'Suddenly everything began to darken. As though the night were falling — falling in a moment, fast, fast, fast.' He peered up at me, then said with a roughness unusual for him, 'No need for you to wait. Get along to your room. Unpack.'

'I promised Kirsti I'd stay till her return.'

'So much fuss. Those boys gawping at me. That Solomon man turning up the air-conditioning. Dehydration!' Once more lying back against the single hard bolster, he was muttering the words, so that they were all but inaudible. 'It's nothing.'

. . . *It's nothing*. It was not he saying that, but my mother, her hand, cuplike, to her chin. I felt the memory being drawn out from me as though it were a splinter of ice, so long embedded inside me, miraculously frozen, that now to extract it caused an agonizing laceration of all the surrounding tissue. Silent, perched on the edge of the bed, I stared down at my father, whose eyes once more were shut. The splinter of ice began to thaw.

In a room of the mean Delhi bungalow, overlooking an untidy garden, the neat, compact man, with the handsome, overlarge head, was tapping away at the typewriter, the ribbons of which his wife would always change for him. The seven-year-old boy was playing with a child's tennis racket and ball, hitting the ball against the wall of the bungalow and then, as it bounced back, hitting it once more, with that unerring eye that was to make him so successful a games player at both preparatory school and public school.

The man stopped typing, his head appeared at the window. He never spoke angrily to the boy, however angry, as now, his feelings. 'Oh, Rupert, do go and play on the other side of the house, there's a good chap. I'm trying to work, something important, you see, and it's awfully hard to concentrate with that noise of the ball and of your feet on the gravel.'

Without saying anything, the boy picked up the ball and, kicking sulkily at the gravel, slowly made his way over to the other side of the house. His mother, resting on her bed, heard him, got off it, and came to the french windows. She was small, thin, elegant even in bare feet and a Japanese silk kimono too large for her, which she had snatched up off the end of the bed and wrapped quickly around her.

'Daddy says I mustn't play on that side of the house. It disturbs his writing, he says.'

'Well, play on this side, then.'

'Then I'll disturb you.'

'That doesn't matter. I was just lying there, not sleeping.'

'But the doctor said you must rest every afternoon. Didn't he?'

'He's an old fusspot.' This doctor was not the young Canadian missionary of two years later, but a bleary-eyed, spongy-faced Irishman, who always expected to be offered a glass of whisky after a call. 'Would you like to try the bicycle again?' For his birthday, two days before, his parents had given him what was then called 'a fairy cycle'. He had still not mastered it.

'If you don't want to rest, Mummy.'

'I've had enough of resting. Plenty of time to rest in the grave.' (Had she really said that, or were the words merely the result of the workings of what my father would call 'creative memory', when catching me out in some divergence from the literal truth?) 'You get the bike, I'll be with you in a moment — just as soon as I've slipped into a frock and some shoes.'

Carefully the boy wheeled the shiny new bicycle from the shed, with its roof of rusty corrugated iron, its huge spiders in webs that swayed back and forth in the draught created by the opening of the door, and its smells of mould and, inexplicably since none was near it, of drains.

His mother came out through the french windows in a simple, white cotton dress, low at the neck, so that her collarbones were visible in pathetic prominence. 'Here I am, darling!' She had always had about her a hectic gaiety, which he had only recognized later in his life as a classic symptom of her illness. 'Get on!' She put one hand to the saddle of the bicycle and the other to the handlebars. 'That's right. Now hold on tight to the handlebars. And put your feet on the pedals. Both pedals.' He could smell her scent, as sweet as the scent of the purple flowers of the creeper that covered the porch but with a bitterness underlying that sweetness, just as, two years later, riding on another bicycle, this time as a passenger, he was to smell the healthy sweat of the Canadian missionary. 'Now, away we go! Pedal! Go on — pedal!'

He pedalled furiously, leaning over the handlebars, so that his cheek almost touched her hand, his face screwed up in a determined frown and his legs working like pistons.

'That's it, that's it!' she cried out. 'You're getting it now. Go on! Go on!'

They incised a circle on the gravel once, twice, three times. She was laughing in delight at their success, right hand now off the handlebars and left hand merely resting on the saddle as a safety precaution. 'Yes, yes, yes!'

Then all at once she halted abruptly, attempting to keep control of the bicycle with the child still astride it. But it moved out of her grasp as she began to cough, careered sideways, tipped over. The boy lay sprawled on the gravel, looking up at the woman, who was now bent almost double, her body shaken with coughing and her hand raised cuplike to her mouth. She made a retching sound, her eyes fixed, at once terrified and beseeching, on him. Then the blood spurted, effortlessly so it seemed to the boy, out over her lower lip and into her hand. She turned away, equally horrified that this thing should have happened to her and that he should have witnessed its happening.

Although one of his elbows and a shin were grazed, he jumped up off the gravel and ran after her, as she hurried into the house. 'Mummy, what is it? What is it?'

Her head averted from him, her back oddly arched, she said thickly, as though still through the blood, 'It's nothing.'

It's nothing. Her words and my father's words, spoken more than twenty years later, now clicked together decisively, like the press studs of a belt. The belt was all at once confining my spirit.

What that neat, compact man, with the overlarge, handsome head, had been typing when he had looked out of the window and, courtesy masking his anger, had asked me to go and play somewhere else, I have no idea. Perhaps it was the novel about India that he had told me that he had once started and then abandoned because 'E.M. Forster seemed to me to have said it all already.' Perhaps it was that book about architecture, about which I was never to learn anything but its title, *Frozen Music.* At all events, it had not mattered that the boy with the tennis racket and ball had moved away out of earshot, any more than it had mattered that the woman, disobeying her Swiss specialist's advice, had insisted on accompanying him out to the country in which she was to die. Both the small sacrifice and the huge one had been equally barren. The sun was sinking and the tasks in the garden would never be completed.

He opened his eyes and looked up into mine. 'Why are you staring at me like that?' There was a note both of panic and of anger in his voice. By what miracle had he intuited, eyes shut, that I had been staring down at him, superimposing on the grey, lined face, with the hectic spot on each cheekbone, the fuller, smoother, healthier face that had appeared, so many years ago now, at the window of the mean Delhi bungalow?

'Was I staring? I was thinking, that's all. My thoughts were miles away — years away.'

'So were mine,' he said surprisingly. But he did not elaborate.

Kirsti returned. 'There's still the Canadian mission. But there's no longer any doctor. Just the one man — Vellacott, I think Solomon said.'

'Yes, Vellacott,' my father said dreamily. I guessed that his temperature must now be high. 'I remember Vellacott. Decent man. Bit of a prig. But decent.'

I had risen from the bed. Kirsti now seated herself on it, once again taking my father's hand in her own. 'An Indian doctor's coming. Solomon says he's good — "top class" was how he put it. He worked in England for a while. He's called da Costa. That doesn't sound Indian, does it?'

'Goanese.' Then my father added, 'The best cooks come from Goa. I hope he's not going to cook my goose.' His laughter at his own silly little joke gurgled at the back of his cruelly inflamed throat.

Kirsti got up. 'Now I'm going to take your temperature.' She crossed over to the smaller of her suitcases. I knew that tone, the tone of a professional nurse. She rarely used it, but when she did, it meant that there was to be no arguing with her. My father also knew it. He did not argue.

Since she packs with the same orderliness that she has lived her whole life, she had no difficulty in locating first her leather-covered medicine chest and then, inside the medicine chest, a thermometer in a shiny metal tube.

As my father lay back in sulky resignation, the thermometer under his tongue, Kirsti turned to me. 'Don't you want to go along to your room?' It was as though she wished to keep his temperature a secret even from me.

'Let's see what it is first.'

She peered at the thermometer, holding it up to the light filtering through the shuttered window. 'As I thought.'

'How much is it?' my father asked.

'More than it should be.' Again she made it clear that she would prefer me to go. 'Do see to your room. I'll tell you what the doctor says.'

'Is there nothing I can do?'

She smiled at me, head on one side, with a singular sweetness. 'Nothing. Thank you, Rupert. Philip had better sleep. And I'll write up my diary. I'm behind with it.'

Once she had left this diary out on the table at which we had been sitting in the garden of our Agra hotel, while she went in to see if my father had woken from his siesta. Surreptitiously I had opened it and looked inside, hoping to discover something exciting, perhaps even disreputable, about this woman who had already begun to elbow out of my mind that once constant image of the wife who had left me. But all it contained were lists, written out in a hand as neat, clear and bold as its author. Food eaten. Miles covered. Relative temperatures. Temples visited. Palaces visited. Caves visited. Costs of souvenirs. Costs of drinks, meals, rooms. Surely there was more to her than all these trivial, external circumstances, recorded with so much scrupulousness?

When I arrived at the reception desk to tell Solomon that I was now ready to be shown to my room, there was a man standing there, a smart attaché case with a combination lock in one hand, whom I at once knew to be Dr da Costa. He was wearing not the usual trousers and open-necked shirt of educated Indians, but a beige raw-silk suit and a dark-brown raw-silk tie. He was beautifully shod in moccasins, and wore glasses with heavy steel frames, which I guessed to be imported from Germany. Behind an initial impression of softness one felt the strength of his personality, just as his at first yielding palm grew firm as I held it in my grip.

Like many doctors, he did not wish to hear my father's or Kirsti's diagnosis of what might be wrong. He did not seem even to wish my father to enumerate his symptoms. It was only when Kirsti used the word 'pyrexia' that he paid her any attention, looking up startled from his examination of my father's throat. He was not to know of her past career in nursing.

Eventually he rose from the edge of the bed, removing his stethoscope. 'A streptococcal infection of the throat. Common among visitors to India. I'll write a prescription for some antibiotics. One of the hotel boys can take it to the chemist. And have him gargle with salt and water. Yes, just that, salt and water. The best thing.'

As he perched on the window-ledge, the prescription pad on his upraised knee, Kirsti asked, 'What do we owe you, Dr da Costa?'

He looked up and said curtly, 'Forty rupees.'

'Forty rupees!' Like me, Kirsti was astounded by the smallness of the sum.

'Yes, forty rupees.' Having finished writing out the prescription, he began to screw the top back onto his old-fashioned fountain pen. 'That, I am afraid, is what I charge my Indian patients.'

Kirsti was embarrassed. 'It wasn't that it seemed too much,' she said. 'It seemed far too little.'

'Yes, it is far too little. But it's what I charge my Indian patients. So I must charge you the same.'

'Oh, but we'd be happy to –' Kirsti began.

He cut her off brusquely. 'Forty rupees.'

Kirsti removed the money from her bag. 'We're terribly grateful.' She held it out.

Taking the notes without a word of thanks, he stuffed them into the top pocket of his jacket. Then he said, 'If there's no improvement by tomorrow, get Mr Solomon to call me again. But I don't think that'll be necessary.'

After I had unpacked in my small, stark but welcomingly clean room, I went back to my father and Kirsti. Kirsti opened the door to my knock, a finger to her lips. 'He's taken the first dose and now he's asleep.'

'Now that it's cooler, I thought of going out. What are you going to do?'

She looked surprised, even shocked by the question. 'Stay with him, of course.'

In my annoyance that she should prefer to sit in the small, inadequately air-conditioned room with my sleeping father rather than explore the town with me, I wanted to tell her,

'He's not dying, you know.' But I merely said, 'Yes, of course. Is there anything else he needs?'

'I don't think so. I've asked Rajiv to buy him some mineral water — they don't seem to have any here. And some bananas — for some reason he has a craving for bananas, though usually, as you know, he doesn't like them.'

When I passed through the lobby, Mr Solomon was far more loquacious and friendly than at our arrival. 'How is your dad?' he asked as I handed him my room key.

'Sleeping.'

'Dr da Costa is a very good man. You can have absolute confidence in him. No fear.'

'Yes, he seemed very capable.'

'He does not have to work. His father is a rich man, a merchant. Dr da Costa could have worked in England. But he came back here to Balram.' As I turned away, he continued, 'So your uncle was Mr Reynolds?'

'That's right. My mother's brother.'

He laughed, plump hands on ample hips, his jowls shaking. 'My dad was frightened of Mr Reynolds. I used to say to him — I was only a young lad at the time — "Dad," I used to say, "Dad, why are you so frightened of Mr Reynolds? Soon Mr Reynolds and all the other burra sahibs will be swept out of India." But my dad remained scared, always scared.'

'I was frightened of him too.'

'*You?*' He was incredulous.

'I was only a child.'

'Yes, of course, you were only a child. But how could a grown man like my dad be in a state of constant blue funk over what Mr Reynolds might say or think? I ask you!'

He asked me, I had no answer.

On an impulse, I now asked Mr Solomon to direct me to

the Canadian mission. He pulled a notepad towards him, leant on the counter and began to draw me a map in pencil. Then he stopped, to look up and say, 'You have your driver. Why don't you take him? Much easier.'

'Oh, he's probably having a siesta.'

'Never mind! This boy' — he pointed to the boy silently watching and listening to us, as he leant against the wall by the staircase — 'can go and wake him. Easy.'

'No, no. Let him sleep.'

'You mustn't spoil these chaps. They don't understand spoiling, not at all.'

I could see that there was no chance of his spoiling his boys.

Although it was past five o'clock, about the same time that we had passed through Balram on our first, fleeting visit, the air was still burning. I stood for a while under the tattered awning by the entrance, while the beggar, his shrivelled leg still stuck out before him and his crutch still lying beside him, pleaded hoarsely, 'Sahib! Sahib! Baksheesh!' Eventually I felt in my trouser pocket and threw down some coins. The last time that I had thrown down coins like that my father had reproached me. 'Oh, don't throw down money like that, Rupert! Put it in his hand. It's so brutal to throw it down like that.' If it was now brutal, I felt brutal and wanted it to be brutal.

The half-naked mechanics were now drifting back to their work from their siestas, always in groups of three, four or five. I thought, as I had so often thought in India, that it was extraordinarily rare ever to see anyone alone by choice. One or two of the mechanics stared at me, as they would not have done in some tourist centre like Agra, Delhi or Jaipur. I should guess that it was unusual for anyone white to visit Balram, which was mentioned in the guidebooks only because of its nearby fort and palace.

I looked at Mr Solomon's map once again, and then began to walk. But either he had not drawn it properly or I did not follow it properly, since soon I was lost. From the main road, crowded with cars, carts and pedestrians, I turned into a narrow road, with stalls on either side of it, a cow ruminating in a dry gutter, and some monkeys chattering high up in the trees that threw their shadows over a stagnant pond where some pot-bellied, completely naked children were bathing. From the narrow road I turned off into one even narrower, little more than a path, with another gutter, this time glittering with water, beside it. I looked down into the gutter and, as I did so, a huge turd floated past. I heard my uncle say, far back in the past, 'It's a dung economy. Animal dung, human dung. Dung fuels not only their cooking stoves but their lives. They fertilize their fields with it, they build their houses from it. When they die, it's a case not of "Earth to earth" but "Dung to dung".'

Somewhere, I could not see where, a bird was singing. I turned my face upwards to the trees and to the still blazing sky revealed through the interstices of their branches, and looked everywhere for it, as its song showered down onto my cheeks, eyelids and lips. The moment was one of those islands of ravishing beauty that, in India, constantly emerge from a sea of, well, dung.

Yes, I was lost. But it did not seem to matter. I walked on. If I saw a taxi, a motor rickshaw or even a horse-drawn carriage, I would take it. If not, there was the road before me, and there was the evil-smelling gutter beside me. Perhaps, if I was lucky, that bird would once again trill with effortless virtuosity somewhere above me.

All at once I saw it, in the distance, across what appeared to be a vast scrapyard, scattered metal glittering, no doubt so hot that one could not touch it, in the afternoon glare. It tilted slightly to the right, just as I remembered it. The Leaning Spire of Balram. But, like everything recalled from childhood, it now looked much smaller, a model, no more, of something that had once existed. I began to walk towards it through the junked cars, bicycles, iceboxes, cooking stoves, even though there was a notice in Hindi with, below it, in English: 'Private. Keep out.'

As I stood at the open gates of the mission, staring through them, I saw that the garden, in which Clive Vellacott and I had played our noisy, ferocious games, often coming to blows, had also strangely shrivelled. Could that really be the high, precipitous bank, now no more than a gentle slope extending the short distance from a clump of trees to a flowerbed choked with weeds, down which we had rolled with excited squeals of pleasure? Could that really be the banyan tree, its branches proliferating over acres so it had seemed, among which we would hide both from each other and from the adults? I felt first a wonder, then fear. The cruellest of all betrayals is this kind of betrayal by memory.

I had intended to go up the drive, ring the bell and ask to see Mr Vellacott. But now I had no heart for it. Another time. With my father, with Kirsti.

I turned away. Then, abruptly, as though an invisible hand had tugged at me, I turned back. I had forgotten to look for Jack Mackenzie's bungalow, with that room full of radio equipment and all those impatient patients waiting outside. I stared. The bungalow simply was not there. There was no trace of it. What had happened to it? Had it been burned down? Removed, brick by brick, to some other place? Or had

the 'creative memory' of which my father so often accused me built me the bungalow, put the kitchen table inside its sitting room, covered that kitchen table with the two receivers, the loudspeaker, the transformer and the jumble of wires and random parts, and then set down, on either side of it, a large, freckled, sweating Canadian and a small, sturdy English boy, his hair cut in a blond fringe across his sunburned forehead?

I heard that voice say, 'Sure?', and then my own voice, childishly treble, answer with precisely the same transatlantic accent: 'Sure.' Could it be that neither of those two voices had ever really said that word at that time in that place?

'I don't know if I ought really to leave him.'

'Oh, come on! You say his temperature's going down.'

'Going down. Not gone down.'

I felt exasperated by Kirsti's devotion to my father, as to a mortally sick child. 'Before he married you, he looked after himself perfectly well when he was ill. My aunt certainly wasn't going to look after him. It was enough to get her to look after the house. And it's not as though there were anything seriously wrong.'

Kirsti frowned, torn between the two possible decisions, between my father and me.

'He has a bell next to his bed. We can ask Solomon to look in to see if he's all right. He spends all his time sleeping anyway. So he doesn't need any company.'

Again Kirsti frowned, staring down at the concrete floor of the corridor. 'Oh, all right,' she said at last, as though she were doing me a good turn against her better judgement. 'I'll just go in and tell him.'

She left the bedroom door ajar, so that I could hear her voice, too low for me to make out what she was saying, and then my father's, much louder, interrupting, 'But of course you must go. No use wasting your time in India by a sickbed. But don't go and see the Melavadi palace. Wait for me to do that. I particularly want to see it again. It's so clear in my memory after all these years. The maharani took a shine to Irene and so, when she was having one of her better periods, she and I often used to go out there.'

Eventually Kirsti re-emerged. 'He doesn't seem to mind,' she said in a tone of puzzled regret.

'Of course not. Why should he mind? What you must realize is that for years and years he's been used to being alone.' I might have added, 'For years and years he preferred to be alone.' Often, when he was planning a visit to the theatre or a holiday or merely setting forth on a walk, I used to say to him, not because I wanted to be with him but because I felt sorry for him, 'Would you like me to come with you?' His usual answer to that would be a sweetly smiling, 'Not unless you really *want* to come. I'm perfectly happy on my own.' I did not really want to come and I knew that he was perfectly happy on his own, and so I did not persist.

In the lobby, her old-fashioned Kodak, once her dead father's, suspended from a shoulder, Kirsti said, 'Well, where are we going?'

I laughed. 'I've no idea. If the palace is out, there's nothing else in the guidebook.' Suddenly an idea came to me. 'I know! I want to see the house where my uncle lived — where my mother died. Or would that bore you?'

'No, of course it wouldn't bore me. But oughtn't we to wait until Philip is up again? He's sure to want to go there.'

Although I could not have said why, I did not want to share with my father my first view of that house, once so dim in my memory but now, with each hour that we spent in

Balram, becoming sharper and sharper, like some ancient recording recovering its pristine bloom in the process of being transferred to digital disc. The house – or, rather, the memory of the house – was mine and also, in an eerie way, my dead mother's. I felt a passionate, secret jealousy that he might appropriate even a part of it. 'We can make a preliminary reconnoitre. Why not? Then if he wants to see it, we can go again.'

'Perhaps it no longer exists.'

Yes, perhaps, like Jack Mackenzie's bungalow, it no longer existed. Perhaps – the strange fancy again came to me, as with the bungalow – it had never existed except in my mind.

'How do we get there?'

I felt relief that, in a subtle way, she had now sided with me, not with my father. 'I'll ask Solomon.'

Mr Solomon was clearly dubious about our going there at all. 'Why do you want to go there?' I thought the reason obvious. 'The house is completely changed. You will not recognize it.'

'Yes, but I'd be interested to see it again. We stayed there for several weeks with my uncle.' I realized only then that I did not know how many weeks it had been. To a child it had seemed an eternity of happiness, darkened only intermittently by the growing awareness of my mother's illness in that shadowy room, its blinds drawn down against the sunlight, with eventually at least one of two Eurasian nurses, Jessie and Betty, in constant attendance on her. 'My mother died there,' I added, deciding to reveal to him what I had previously concealed.

'Yes, I know.' How did he know? Perhaps since our arrival he had been talking about these relatives of Mr Reynolds to old cronies of his now dead father. 'But you must understand, there are now many families living in that house. It is still a railway house but there are three, four railway families there. Engineers, educated people, you understand. But they share the house.'

'Well, I think we'd like to go. How do we get there?'

'You will take your car?'

I looked at Kirsti. 'Might as well,' she said. Rajiv was in the lobby behind us, awaiting his orders. Not at all the solemn, anxious Rajiv whom we knew, he was joking with the two boys on duty, sending them into squeals of laughter.

Mr Solomon drew in a deep gulp of air, his mouth wide open to reveal the two gold cappings. 'Very well.' He might have been reluctantly agreeing to our keeping a dog in one of our rooms or all sleeping in the same bed. Looking over to Rajiv, he summoned him with a peremptory click of the fingers. We would never have dreamed of summoning Rajiv like that.

In English he began to explain how to reach St Leonards. I had forgotten that that had been the name of the house, painted, white on dark green, on the gate before the gravel drive. It was odd that, long after the departure of the British, a dinky South Coast resort should still be commemorated on this vast subcontinent.

Behind the Balram through which we had driven and through which, the day before, I had walked, there was a humped, green hill. As we drove towards it, I began to realize why, when we had first entered the town, my father had insisted that 'the real Balram' was attractive. The narrow, ill-smelling streets, lined with stalls lit at night by naphtha, the often unfinished concrete buildings, rusty iron rods sticking up from them like a forest of television aerials, the stunted trees, the cracked paving stones, the makeshift shacks constructed of old packing cases and corrugated iron, the half-naked, pot-bellied children, the importunate beggars with their hideous deformities, the jostling people struggling for life like fish gasping for air in an over-crowded pool drained of all but a shallow inch or two of its water: perhaps all these things were merely some hideous illusion, and all that was real was the small, green suburb built for the occupancy of a ruling class.

The road was wide and there were no cattle straying across it. Some of the gardens behind gates with names like Balmoral, Woodlands, The Croft and Mount Pleasant inscribed on them, were sadly overgrown, but some were beautiful in their lavish, garish colours. 'It is near here,' Rajiv said, 'that we must pass the *maidan*. Then the main post office.' I could remember the *maidan* but nothing of the post office, although I must often have passed it. Rajiv peered again at the map drawn for him by Mr Solomon on the back of a buff business envelope.

Kirsti and I had been sitting silent beside each other all through the drive. But I felt as if our bodies, although they never made even a fleeting contact, were carrying on some kind of tense, tentative conversation with each other, every nerve alert.

Now she broke the silence. 'Why did your uncle call the house St Leonards?'

'I don't think he did call it that. Someone long before he ever arrived in Balram probably did so.'

'It's strange — and rather sad — to think of that someone coming out here years and years ago, probably long before either of us was born, to feel so much homesickness for St Leonards that he chose that name for his house. Who was St Leonard anyway?'

'I've no idea.'

'We have arrived, sahib.' Rajiv would never have thought of announcing, 'We have arrived, memsahib,' any more than he would ever have thought of asking Kirsti for directions as to where next he was to take us.

The paint on the gate had so much peeled that all that I could decipher was 'St Leo . . .'. The gravel drive, where I would often pass the two gardeners squatting, naked but for loincloths, as they excavated and tugged up the weeds with their bare hands, was now covered in a greenish-yellow rash. On the left side of this drive, where there had once been a lawn, there now stretched what looked like two abandoned allotments, separated from each other and from the drive by festoons of barbed wire resembling huge, rusty balls of knitting wool. On the right side, it was still possible to see that there had once been a tennis court.

On the late afternoon after the night during which my mother had died, the two nurses Jessie and Betty had gone out on to the tennis court to hit a ball slackly back and forth between them, while, lying on my stomach on the grass, my chin cupped in my hands, I had watched them. Then my uncle had rushed out of the house and shouted at the dark, angular girls, 'Have you no sense of decency? Have you no human feelings? Playing tennis on this of all days!' Without saying a word, without even picking up the ball, the girls, terrified and humiliated, at once scurried back, heads lowered, into the house. I had scrambled to my feet. My uncle now came over to me and, having put an arm round my shoulder, said in a totally different voice, grieving and gentle, 'Come inside. Come inside with me.'

Now, on this area, a seesaw had been set up, with one small child, a girl, sitting astride it, and another, a boy, standing near. The children wore identical white shoes, with straps across the insteps, and beautifully laundered white clothes. They might have been about to pose for a detergent advertisement. A pedal car, one wheel missing, lay on its side near to them.

The house behind them, its once immaculate façade scarred and pocked where the stucco had come away to reveal the raw brick behind it, had – need I say it? – shrunk, so that what had previously been a mansion in my memory had become the sort of Edwardian bungalow that might indeed be found in St Leonards.

Both of us were peering out from the car, from which Rajiv had already alighted. He put a hand to the door beside me and left it there, strangely hesitant, before eventually opening it for me. 'Do you want to get out, sahib?' He said it as though he expected me to say no.

Should I ask him to drive us through the gate, which was hanging half open, and up to the house, in the manner of my uncle's Sikh driver, resplendent in his maroon uniform, with the gold braid on its cuffs and round its collar, and in his turban, a kind of outsize teacosy, with the insignia of the railway on it? No, I decided, we had better walk.

'Let's go on foot,' I said to Kirsti, clambering out.

'Yes,' she agreed. 'Much better.'

The children, clearly Eurasian, watched us, motionless and silent, as we crunched past them. Both had the same beautiful colouring, the ivory of a cigarette holder faintly stained with nicotine, as had Mr Singh at the hotel which had failed to find us rooms in Indore. Both had extremely long necks and extremely thin legs and arms, making them look pathetically fragile.

There was no bell. There never had been one, I remembered. When visitors arrived in the past, they would open first the front door, which was never locked, and then the wire-netting door within it, and shout out something like 'Anyone at home?' to bring a servant running. I wondered whether I should open the door now and shout out like those visitors of some twenty years ago, 'Anyone at home?' I decided to knock. No one answered. I knocked again.

Eventually a woman, darker than the children but with the same fragile beauty, came to the door. She was wearing feathered mules, of a kind that I could remember my mother wearing, and a flowered silk kimono, which she was holding about her with one hand for lack of a sash. Her hair was in rollers. 'Yes?' The question was indolent, incurious.

I explained the purpose of our errand. Once, long ago, as a child, I had lived here, and once, long ago, my mother had died here. Would it be possible for us to look around?

'You can look over our quarters, if you wish.' She was neutral, neither friendly nor unfriendly. We might have been prospective purchasers who had arrived without a prior warning from an estate agent. 'But I know that Mrs Taylor is out, she has gone down to the market, and the Owens are out too.'

'They live in the other — flats?' I was not sure what to call them.

'That's right. My hubby works on the railway. So do Mr Taylor and both the Owens.'

'It's a railway house, isn't it?'

'That's right.'

'My uncle worked on the railway. We were staying with him.' Should I tell her that my uncle had been managing director of the railway? Better not. In any case, she clearly had no interest in learning anything further about either him or us.

'I don't know exactly what it is you want to see.'

Turning her back to us, she retreated into the cavernous hall behind her. Kirsti and I followed.

'Oh, we just want to look around,' I said, remembering how this bare space had once had ranged round its walls the heads of animals that my Uncle Claud had shot. The floor was covered with linoleum, in a pattern of large deep-pink roses on a pale-pink ground. A child's doll lay out on it, abandoned. She stooped with a sigh, picked it up and threw it onto a Formica-topped table.

'I'd better introduce myself. My name is Mrs Watts.'

I had already told her our names. 'Mrs Watts,' I repeated.

'We have four rooms. You must excuse the untidiness. The girl is sick, some kind of enteric, and the boy has gone on an errand for my hubby. You saw my children?'

'Yes. How beautiful they are,' Kirsti said.

For the first time Mrs Watts smiled.

She put a hand to a door, releasing the edge of her kimono so that it fell away to reveal that, underneath, she was wearing nothing but brassiere and knickers. Embarrassed, she snatched at the edge and pulled it back. 'This is the parlour,' she said. It was an odd word to hear used out in India.

The room, which had been — yes, suddenly I realized it — my mother's sickroom, looked, apart from its high ceiling and its greater size, almost exactly like a parlour in some lower-middle-class home back in England. There were lumpish chairs and a sofa, all covered in the same flowered cretonne, innumerable small tables, a brass pot containing a straggling fern, a bookcase with tattered back numbers of the *Reader's Digest* ranged sparsely in it, and an upright piano, its mahogany veneer chipped. The only difference from a parlour back in England was the electric fan above us, its former white yellowed in streaks.

. . . Round and round it creaked, hypnotic to the little boy who lay on his mother's bed, her arm around him. That was the last time he was allowed that proximity. After that, he had been forbidden to go too close. Indeed, during her last weeks, he had had to speak to her through the window. 'Why, why, why?' he had asked in tearful rage at this exclusion, and his father had then told him gently, 'Dr Mackenzie thinks it best. You see, you might catch this nasty bug that Mummy has. We don't want that, do we? We don't want you ill as well as her.'

She held me very close, a hand, on which the rings were now so loose that I feared they might fall off, gripping my forearm. Then Jessie — Betty had not yet joined the household — came in with a tray. 'I must give you your injection, Mrs Ramsden. And take your temp.' I could hear, with Kirsti and Mrs Watts beside me, that plaintively sing-song voice, not unlike Mrs Watts's own.

The dying woman sighed beside the small child and relinquished her grip. 'Yes, run along, darling. Run along and enjoy yourself.'

I ran along, out into the scorching sun of the garden. I knew, for the first time, that something terrible was happening. But I had no idea of its nature.

There was a swing dangling from a tree beside the tennis court. It had been put there, not for me, but for my two cousins, my uncle's prim, brainy children, a boy and a girl, now back 'home' with their mother in England. I sat on it and, still fearful, though I could not have said why, I swung myself slowly back and forth.

All at once I heard that Canadian voice: 'Hi!'

Jack alighted from his bicycle and wheeled it towards me over the grass. 'Are you the only one around?'

I nodded. 'Except for Jessie.' I never thought of including the servants, who lived lives so separate from ours that, like some other species, they exerted over me a compelling but wary fascination.

'I was passing, so I thought I'd look in to see how your mother was getting on.' Earlier that day, in the morning, he had already called to see her.

'What . . .?' I began and then broke off, my throat closing with the apprehension of something still undefinable.

'Yes?' He looked down at me, smiling but oddly sad.

'What's wrong with mummy?'

Again he smiled, in attempted reassurance, and again I was aware, with the ready intuition of a child, of a sadness, even desolation. 'Nothing that we can't put right. Don't worry.'

But he was worried. I knew that he was worried. I stared up at him, as I still swung gently back and forth, until his clear blue eyes shifted sideways and downwards. 'Well, I'd better go in. I've a lot of calls still to make.' He began to wheel his bicycle towards the front door. His shoulders were slumped, his head was tilted forward. He looked exhausted by more than those patients seen and still to see.

. . . Now, in this room in which my mother had first lived for so many weeks of alternating hope and despair and had then died, I tilted my head back once more to gaze up at the fan. Day after day, it had creaked round and round above her, as though shifting some invisible weight. Now it was still.

Kirsti had raised the lid of the upright piano, as she and Mrs Watts chatted to each other. Where were we staying? Yes, that was a nice hotel, the nicest in Balram, and Mr Solomon was such a nice gentleman, always ready with a friendly word or a friendly action. Kirsti played a chord, plangent and poignant in the room which was only partly the room which I had known.

'Oh, do you play?' Mrs Watts asked.

'Once. Not now.'

'My daughter Violet plays beautifully. We think one day she'll be a concert pianist. I'll call her. You must hear her.'

She went to the window through which I had so often talked to my mother, my hand nudging aside the blind. As she threw back shutters which had not, I was sure, existed in my uncle's day, the light, white and hot, exploded against her. She leant far out, calling in a high, sing-song voice, 'Vi! Vi! Vi!'

Eventually the little girl, her glossy black hair parted in the middle and tied in two bows, sidled into the room. She gave a little shy curtsey first to Kirsti and then to me, before she danced rather than walked over to the piano. Her mother nodded and gave us a proud smile which irradiated her face, like that sunlight which had exploded against it. 'Play the Beethoven,' she told the child. 'The Sonatina.'

Although the piece is one given, sooner or later, to almost every beginner, it was strange that it should now be played in the house in which, so many years before, I myself had played it. The child, her dangling legs too short to reach the pedals, bent her head and struck the keys. She executed the admittedly easy piece with what struck me as a faultless artistry.

At a grand piano, tuned by an elderly man once, improbably, a confectioner, I used to sit, not in this room but in the drawing room, with Pattie beside me. She would lean her fresh, eager face towards the music propped up before us, no less bored than I was and no less eager to get away. When my father had first engaged Pattie as my governess, it was on the understanding that she must include music among the subjects that she taught me. But she had neither the proficiency nor the taste for music of this sort, preferring to play records of Jack Payne or Harry Roy on the wind-up gramophone which, she had once confided to me, had been a present from a soldier boyfriend, now posted back to England.

My mother, when still well enough to move about the house, would look in on us during these sessions, her whole body from time to time shaken by a paroxysm of coughing. 'The blind leading the blind,' she remarked on one occasion, not of course in Pattie's hearing. 'The tone-deaf leading the tone-deaf,' my father amended. But he obstinately insisted that the lessons should continue.

There was a grave beauty about both the girl herself and her pellucid playing. Kirsti had seated herself on the sofa, I had seated myself beside her. By accident — it could only have been by accident, I decided — her leg touched mine, moved away, returned. She smelled clean and fresh in a country in which most people, Indian or foreign, smelled frowsty and sour.

The child finished and turned round, with a small, self-satisfied smile, for our approbation. Kirsti raised her hands in the air and clapped, 'Bravo!'

'That was good,' I said. 'Very good.'

The girl jumped off the stool and gave another little curtsey, similar to the ones she had given us on entering.

'We don't know from whom she gets her gift. Her dad doesn't play and neither do I.'

Mrs Watts showed us the other rooms — an untidy, stuffy bedroom, once my uncle's study but now almost entirely filled with a huge, sagging double bed, a small, boxlike sitting room, once my father's bedroom, another room given over to the children, whose toys and clothing littered the floor. But I felt a sudden weariness, I was no longer interested. After this tour of inspection, she insisted on 'knocking up' — her phrase — the other two families. But fortunately in each case no one answered her repeated calls.

'It was kind of you to let us see over everything,' Kirsti said. 'And to let us have the opportunity to hear your daughter. We shan't forget that.' She spoke with the simplicity and sincerity that always at once won her friends.

Having followed dutifully in our wake, the little girl now slipped away from us without a word or even a glance, to rejoin her brother whom I could see perched motionless on the seesaw, staring out into space, as though in a deliberate refusal to stare at us. Mrs Watts took my hand in her soft, yielding one. 'Please feel free to look around the garden.'

What garden? I thought but did not say. There was no longer any garden. What had been the garden was now half wilderness and half rubbish tip.

Leaving the two women, I walked over the gravel to what had once been the window of my mother's bedroom. Mrs Watts had once again closed the shutters, there was no way of looking in except through the slats. I put my hand on the window-ledge, as the little boy used to do.

. . . 'Is that you, darling?'

'When are you going to get up, Mummy?'

'When Dr Mackenzie tells me it's safe for me to do so.'

Then the little boy felt that it was Dr Mackenzie who was keeping this frail, effervescent woman prisoner in the darkened room. 'How does Dr Mackenzie know when it's safe for you to get up?'

'Because he's such a clever doctor.' Then she added, as though she had only then thought it, 'And such a good man.'

. . . It was many days later. Once again the little boy looked through the window, a grubby hand pushing the blind to one side. He could see a broad back, completely obscuring the woman beyond it. The sweat was making the doctor's cotton shirt stick to his back. He was lying across the bed.

. . . It was many more days later. Again the little boy looked through the window. His mother lay back on the high-piled pillows, with something — tears? could it be tears? he had never seen her cry — glistening on cheekbones high above sunken-in cheeks. The doctor sat in the armchair in which the boy's father also sat when visiting his wife after a long day away from home. He was away now. The doctor had covered his face with those large hands, freckled, the reddish hair thick on them. He had covered his face. Why? What was he trying to hide?

. . . Suddenly I felt Kirsti's fingers on my shoulder. 'Let's go,' she said, in a hurried, hushed voice. It was as though she were afraid that someone, somewhere might still be watching us.

Rajiv drove us on to a grocer's shop housed in an airless corrugated-iron building that from the outside looked like a garage, where we bought food, mostly tinned, for our lunch. Kirsti had brought with her from England a picnic basket, with plastic crockery, and cutlery so light that it too might have been made of plastic. Each night, with her usual efficiency, she would carefully wash and dry whatever we had soiled. She also had a Swiss penknife, which she was obliged to surrender each time that we boarded a plane, to reclaim on arrival. She used this to open bottles and tins and for innumerable other small tasks.

'What did you do this morning?' my father asked, when

we arrived back toting the bags that the grocer had miraculously conjured up for us out of folded newspaper.

Before I could confess the truth to him, Kirsti said, 'Oh, we drove round the town, and then we drove out into the country. Then we had a little walk, until it grew too hot.' I was astonished by the ease of a duplicity that I had never before known her to show.

She began to take the things out of their bags and, pushing anything already on the dressing-table to one side, to lay them out on it. My father watched her, his cheeks still flushed and his eyes still shiny from fever. 'I don't think I want to eat,' he said at last. 'My throat's still sore, and I don't seem to have any appetite.'

'Well, drink some of this apple juice.' Kirsti held up a tin. 'It cost almost as much as a bottle of the local gin.'

'Yes, that would be nice.'

'Would you like some soup? I bought a tin in case. I can warm it up on the primus.'

'No, no soup.'

Silent, as he rarely was when well, my father watched us eat. Under his gaze, I felt a constraint, and could see that Kirsti felt one too. We spoke to each other in abrupt snatches, chiefly to say things like 'This cheese looked awful but it's really not all that bad,' or 'I wonder what Rajiv is eating now' — something we often wondered.

The meal over, Kirsti first wiped the plates clean of any debris into one of the newspaper bags, and then began to wash them and the cutlery at the washbasin. 'I'm sure Solomon doesn't approve of eating in rooms. He gave the bags a distinctly odd glance.'

'Well, someone was certainly cooking in the room next to mine early this morning,' I said. 'I could smell the curry.' I jumped up and snatched the drying-up cloth from Kirsti. 'I'll do that.'

Our task over, my father said, 'What now?'

'We'll sit with you for a little,' Kirsti answered.

'No, no. Don't do that. I'm going back to sleep. That's all I seem to want to do at present. Sleep. Go off somewhere and enjoy yourselves.'

'You can sleep, and I'll sit here and read,' Kirsti insisted.

My father shook his head fretfully. 'Why waste your time in India? Go out, see things, do things.'

I could not help feeling an upsurge of relief and excitement when, with a shrug, Kirsti at last complied.

Out in the corridor, she turned to me. 'Where to?'

Suddenly I had an idea, at once guilty and exciting. Perhaps it was the guilt that made the excitement so intense. 'Why don't we go to the palace? If it still exists.' In this transformed world, it seemed perfectly possible to me that the neo-classical building, designed at the turn of the century not by an architect but by an engineer, had vanished, along with its glasshouses famous for their rare species of cacti.

'All right. Why not?'

In the car, always conscious, as I had been that morning, of that cool, fresh body near to mine, I told her what I remembered of the palace and its inhabitants. There had been the old maharani, her small, crooked teeth stained with *pan*, who had been a staunch friend of my aunt and later of my mother. To my mother, when she was no longer able to move from her room to the garden, much less to the distant palace, she would send brilliantly coloured sweetmeats, invariably handed on to the servants for their children, a crate of champagne and, on one occasion, a brooch made up of a large emerald surrounded by small diamonds, in a fussy Victorian setting.

There had been an argument between my father and my uncle about the brooch. My uncle said that it ought to be returned, since it might be regarded as a bribe. My father laughed at that. 'Why should anyone try to bribe me? I'm not an official, I'm not even a box wallah. I can't do her or her family a single favour.' My uncle replied with the glacial stiffness that was the nearest that he ever got to showing a loss of temper to anyone but Indians, 'I'm not thinking of you, Philip. I'm thinking of myself. I have it in my power to award contracts and to hire and dismiss people. Irene's my sister, as well as your wife.'

But my mother kept the brooch. What later became of it — a question put to me by Kirsti — no one seemed to know. When I once asked my father, he shrugged his shoulders. 'God knows.' If God knew, my father himself had no desire to know. Perhaps, in the aftermath of my mother's death, someone — Jessie, Betty, Pattie, one of the innumerable servants — took it.

The maharani had an unmarried son, whose sole interests in life were the cacti, first assembled by his now dead father, and his stamp collection. Since my uncle also collected stamps, this was a bond between the two men, where otherwise a bond would certainly not have existed.

The maharani's companion was a middle-aged English spinster, a Miss Twelvetrees (like Solomon the name fascinated me and therefore stuck burr-like in my memory), who spoke in a high, shrill, almost hysterical voice, smoked cigarettes through a long amber holder, and, in the view of my parents and uncle, 'slapped on the paint' (the phrase only now comes back to me). The story, told to me not when I was a child but years later by my father, was that Miss Twelvetrees had travelled out to India with what used to be called 'the fishing fleet', that she had landed a Scottish doctor, and that, after their 'marriage', it had all at once been revealed that he already had a wife back in Glasgow. Unable to face an imminent charge of bigamy, he had shot himself.

The old maharajah had left a magnificent stable of horses. These, since the young maharajah rarely rode, were at the disposal of people such as my uncle and aunt and my parents. There was even a piebald pony, mettlesome from too much fodder and too little exercise, on which one of the sayces would from time to time take me out on a leading rein.

The palace, some six miles outside Balram, lay beyond a small village. The road, once asphalted, was bad enough, with its innumerable potholes, before this village was reached. After that, it had so much deteriorated that Kirsti and I constantly found ourselves thrown either against each other or up to the roof. Laughing, Kirsti clutched hold of me with both her hands, crying out, 'Oh, oh, oh!' as the car bumped, lurched and juddered. I had a vague memory of once driving along this same road through the village, but in the opposite direction, in a vast car, a Rolls-Royce or a Daimler, with a pennant flying from its bonnet. I was sitting between the maharani and Miss Twelvetrees, and there were dark blue silk curtains on either side of us, to repel both the sun and prying eyes.

As we drove through a high arch into a courtyard, the once elegant building looked shabby and ramshackle. At the sound of the car, an old man, legs bare and turban soiled and frayed, rose stiffly from where he had been squatting on a low parapet and, wandlike stick in hand, ambled over to us. Rajiv jumped out of the car, in which we were still seated, and explained the purpose of our call. The man shook his head, not vehemently but with a reluctant sadness. Despite what our guidebook said, visitors were clearly not admitted. Rajiv began to argue. Again the melancholy shake of the head. Rajiv turned to us. 'He says palace and garden both shut. Not open to public. If you wish to see, you must write to maharajah.'

'We hardly have time for that.' Since my father was not with us, I had no compunction in pulling out a note. 'Give this to him. See if it does any good.'

The old man examined the note carefully, even turning it over to see the other side. Was he not sure what it was worth? Or did he suspect it to be a forgery? Then, silently, he waved the wandlike stick in the direction of a pair of rusty, padlocked gates at one side of the building.

'Do you wish me to come, sahib?' Rajiv asked.

Although, at least consciously, I had no thought of what was to follow, I said, 'No, that's all right, Rajiv. We'll be back in about an hour.'

The old man disappeared into a shed – who knows, perhaps he lived there – and emerged clutching a huge, rusty key in a gnarled hand. With difficulty he turned it in the padlock on the gate, and with equal difficulty he eventually got the padlock to squeak open. There was another squeak as he tugged the gate towards him. He pointed with the stick. We went through.

This was, so the guidebook told us, 'a garden in the Italian style'. Gravel paths, sprouting weeds, traced concentric circles to enclose flowerbeds in which leggy roses produced a few famished blooms. There was a stone rectangle, once a pool but now full of refuse, in which the tritons no longer spouted water from their conches and the nymphs no longer poured it out from their cornucopias. I looked over my shoulder for the old man, but there was no sign of him.

'Sad, sad, sad,' I said.

'And yet, oddly, it's still beautiful.'

Kirsti was right. 'Yes, it's still beautiful.' Everything – the grass pushing up between the paving stones, the few small roses, the overgrown bushes – glistened miraculously in the light of the late afternoon.

We walked on, leaving the symmetrical parterres, one below the other, to descend to where I remembered the cacti houses to have been. There was an expanse of tall, yellow-green grass, with stone benches set out along it at intervals. A man, head bowed over a book, was sitting on one of these benches, so dishevelled, with his unshaven face and overlong hair, and so shabby, with his flowing white cotton shirt and trousers and his shoes downtrodden at the heels, that one might have mistaken him for a servant. But I knew at once, after so many years, that this was the maharajah.

Although I am sure that he was aware of our presence, at the opposite end of the terrace from himself, he never once looked round. He seemed to be saying silently but fiercely, Don't come near me. Don't talk to me. I don't want to have anything to do with you.

As we moved down to the terrace below, I whispered to Kirsti, 'I'm sure that's the maharajah.'

'Why didn't you speak to him?'

I shrugged.

'I'm sure he'd have liked you to speak to him. After all, you were telling me how fond his mother was of your mother.'

'No, he didn't want me to speak.'

'How do you know that?'

Again I shrugged. How did I know? All I knew was that I knew.

The cacti houses came into view, the sun glittering on the jagged glass of a broken pane on the first and largest of them. The door gaped ajar, half off its hinges. Glass crunched under our feet as we entered. Rack on rack, on either side of us, pots were ranged. But few of the cacti in them still survived. Some of the pots had been knocked over and the sand from them had spilled, gritty and silvery. At the far end, the panes were completely shrouded by a giant creeper, with pale green fleshy leaves and tubular flowers, white at the rim and yellow at the centre, which emitted, as we drew closer and closer, a more and more overpowering smell, sweetish and sickly.

'What is it?' Kirsti asked.

She put out a hand and raised one of the flowers, exploring it with a forefinger. Then bending her head towards her hand, she sniffed at the trumpet. 'It's rather horrible,' she said. The frond fell, seemingly lifeless, from her fingers.

On an impulse, I stepped forward, hearing another splinter of glass crunch under my shoes. I put out one hand to one of her shoulders, then the other hand to the other. She tilted her head back, her spine pressing hard against the edge of the shelf behind her. An elbow knocked over a pot. Then she let out what was half a moan and half a cry. She fell forward towards me, her cheek against my cheek. I pressed closer against her, drew her round, pressed once again, so that now the creeper seemed to be all about us, as we seemed to be all about each other. 'No, no, no.' But after a moment, when she appeared to be struggling to free herself, she gripped me even tighter.

[113]

When at last we moved, my hand in hers as I guided her down through that narrow alleyway of pots full of sand, pots lying on their sides, the sand half trickled out of them, and pots in which dead cacti stood as though charred by some sudden burst of flame, we saw the old man ahead of us, the wandlike stick in his hand. He stared at us out of bleary, expressionless eyes. Then, with what struck me as ironic courtesy, he stepped back to allow us to pass. With the hand that was not in mine, Kirsti was still fumbling at the buttons of her once crisp white blouse, now creased and with a green smear on it, across one breast, where a frond of the creeper had been crushed against it. I could feel the sweat running down my face, and could taste it, bitter on my lips.

'How much did he see?' I asked her as, still hand in hand, we began to climb up to the first of the terraces.

'Everything? Something? Nothing? What does it matter?' Then, after a long pause, she added in a low, constricted voice, 'What really matters is Philip.'

But the terrible thing was that at that moment I did not feel that my father mattered at all.

We sat silent, as though replete after a prolonged banquet, as Rajiv, also silent and his face grim — surely he could not know anything of what had taken place, surely it was only my guilt that made me suspect that he did? — drove us home through the late afternoon sunlight slanting down on the road through the tall trees. Kirsti's hand lay in my lap, mine lay on her thigh. At least Rajiv could not possibly see these contacts.

No doubt, if she had not been lost in some sombre, satiated dream, Kirsti with her unerring sense of direction would have realized that we had taken the road not eastwards back to our hotel, but westwards and therefore out of Balram.

All at once, I had seen them, as I had seen them once before. But this time the elaborate wrought-iron double gates, with 'Protestant' on one and 'Cemetery' on the other, and a Gothic cross fixed high above the letters on each, were on our right and not on our left. 'Look! The cemetery!' I cried out. 'Rajiv! The cemetery!'

'It cannot be the cemetery, sahib,' he said. 'We do not pass the cemetery.' But even as, humiliated once again, he was saying this, he was removing his foot from the accelerator, the brakes were squealing. Looking over his shoulder, he began to back into the cloud of dust raised by our forward passage.

Kirsti leaned across me, her full breasts resting along my forearm, and peered out. 'Yes, it's the cemetery,' she confirmed. 'Oh, never mind. It's not all that far from the hotel.'

'I think I'll get out and have a look.'

'A look at what?'

'The cemetery.' The question struck me as odd. At what else would I want to have a look? I opened the door and put out a leg.

'Oh, no, Rupert! We must wait to go with Philip.'

'Why on earth?'

'It would be a kind of betrayal not to wait to go with him.' It is only now, as I recollect those words, that their full irony stings home to me.

'We needn't tell him.'

'Doesn't secrecy make the betrayal worse?'

A gust of anger whirled through me, because she was right and I did not want her to be right. 'Balls. Tomorrow or the next day – when he's recovered – we can come out here again with him. Why not?'

I began to walk away from the car, the dust dry on my tongue and at the back of my throat. I turned. 'Aren't you going to come too?' She was sitting back in the seat, with an air of tired resignation, her hands folded in her lap. 'Aren't you going to come too?' I repeated.

By now Rajiv had alighted from the car and was standing, turned away from the two of us, his hands on his hips, as — an exercise I had now come to know well — he arched his spine and shook his head rapidly from side to side to relieve his stiffness.

'You go,' she said.

Yes, damn you, I will go! I strode off. To the left of the gate, there was a square concrete house, painted a glittering white, with some plants, recently watered, in petrol drums, also painted white. Some clothes hung motionless in the motionless air, from a line sagging between one stunted tree and another. Someone, presumably a custodian or a gardener, lived there, in a house so much better kept than most houses in Balram. Someone must have washed those clothes and hung them out on that line, and someone must have poured water into the petrol drums. But there was no sign of a soul.

The cicadas, invisible all around me, were deafening as I made my way up the straight, narrow path between the gravestones. Smoke from the sprawling factory beyond the wall had left a dark bruise across the sky. Its bituminous taste was now on my tongue, as well as the dryness of the dust raised by my feet. Crosses had toppled over, stones had been all but obliterated by creepers. As though by a bolt of lightning or by a sword wielded with superhuman power, a stone angel had been split to the waist.

I trudged on. I was sure that I knew where my mother's grave was. I had visited it so often in my dreams that I could not be mistaken. At the far end of the avenue of graves, a ragged boy had come into view, shepherding a herd of lean cows, their udders swinging as they scampered zigzag before him. He was brandishing a wandlike stick, similar to that of the old guardian at the palace. He stopped, stared at me, a hand raised to shield his eyes from the glare, and then, shouting at the cows, ran on.

Dearly beloved daughter of . . . In the bosom of his Maker . . . Departed this life . . . Not lost but . . . From time to time I glimpsed a fragment of some trite, sad sentence, carved there twenty, thirty, forty, fifty, perhaps even a hundred years before. I felt a sudden desolation, weariness, fear.

Eventually I came to a clearing under trees. The grass here had been recently clipped and the two graves, side by side, were free of moss and creepers. I knew at once, I could not have explained why, that one of the graves was my mother's. I walked slowly towards it. Yes. All that was carved on it was 'IRENE RAMSDEN 1907–1938'. Nothing else. That was so like my father, I thought, indulging in no false pieties, sentimentalities or hopes.

For a long time I stared down at the simple letters, incised as though only yesterday on the white stone. Then my attention was attracted by something small moving on the gravestone next to it. I stared. An emerald lizard was attached, tail in air and head down, to the edge of the stone. It was absolutely still but for the rhythmical pulsing of its throat. It was that pulsing that had caught my attention.

As I moved forward, the lizard vanished, as, so many years before, the tree frog had vanished when I had turned in answer to Jack Mackenzie's shout. I looked down at the second gravestone, wondering whose it was. The letters had clearly been carved by the same hand that had carved my mother's stone.

Astonished, I read: 'JACK MICHAEL MACKENZIE. Born

Toronto 1903. Died Balram 1939.' Then gradually it came to me. Jack had died only a few months after my mother. He had been buried here beside her, under an identical tombstone. Someone over the years had tended their twin graves, when almost all the other graves in the cemetery had been cruelly neglected.

I stared down now at one of the inscriptions and now at the other, while far off I heard the factory whistle blowing. Soon the workers would be pouring out, soon the women would be lighting their fires in preparation for the evening meal for their menfolk.

All at once I understood, and, having understood, I almost persuaded myself that, from that far distant time when a lonely, disconsolate child used to nudge aside a blind to peer through his mother's sickroom window, I had always understood.

When I returned to the car, Kirsti was standing some way away from it, as though in a deliberate decision to look neither at the cemetery nor at me. I sensed a tension, as of stretched wire, in her rigid stance. Hands on hips, legs wide apart and head thrown back, she appeared to be gazing across a ravine, goats grazing dispiritedly among its scattered rubbish, to the stark factory chimneys, erupting a yellowish-brown smoke, on the other side. Rajiv was seated at the wheel, the door open beside him and his feet dangling out of it. He had his transistor set on his lap, with a woman singing the Indian equivalent of a Western pop hit in a nasally whining soprano. When he saw me, he at once switched the transistor set off. Kirsti did not turn.

I called. 'Kirsti! I'm back!'

I expected her to ask me about the cemetery – How was it?

Had I found my mother's grave? But those questions were to come later. Now, head lowered, not looking at me, she walked towards the car. She stopped in front of Rajiv.

'Rajiv.'

He looked up, then removed the transistor set from his lap to the seat beside him. 'Yes, memsahib?' He spoke as though afraid of her. But why should that be? She was always courteous and considerate to him, as to every Indian whom we encountered, however exasperating or unlikable.

'I'm going to ask you to do something for me — for us.'

'Yes, memsahib?'

Suddenly he stooped and removed one of his shoes. These shoes, cracked over the insteps and blunted at the toes, appeared to be made of a shiny patent leather but were probably of plastic. One of them still had its original black elastic threaded, in place of a lace, through its eyeholes. The other had a knotted elastic band. It was because of elastic and elastic band that Rajiv could so easily slip the shoes off and on, removing them for driving or for when he was walking on his own, and putting them on again when he was out of the car in our company. He held up the shoe, between him and Kirsti, and inserted an exploratory forefinger into it as though to check if a nail had come through the sole. He peered into the shoe, brows drawn together.

'Please don't tell my husband where we've been today.' Rajiv continued to excavate the shoe with a forefinger, his head now tilted to one side. 'He wants to visit all these places too, and we should have waited for him. But — we were impatient. There seemed to be nothing else to visit in Balram. We don't want to disappoint him.' I sensed her mounting desperation, as Rajiv withheld all response. 'Rajiv?'

At last he looked up. Then, still gazing up at her, he

lowered the shoe and began to push his bare foot into it. 'What you wish, memsahib,' he said.

Now he jumped out of the car — all at once, it struck me that this was the first time that he had ever spoken from a seated position to one of us standing — and opened the door for Kirsti to get into the car.

I clambered in beside her.

She raised her eyebrows in interrogation. I gave a small shrug.

After a surprisingly good dinner, sent in from a restaurant recommended by Mr Solomon, my father and Kirsti played chess, the pocket chess set balanced on the edge of his bed, while I now read one of the English-language newspapers and now pretended to watch the game while really watching her. The line of her back, turned to me so that I could see her face only half in profile, was extraordinarily beautiful in its suppleness and strength.

My father, who played far better than she did, would often gently correct or prompt her as she was about to make a move. Do you really want to do that? Look, my dear, you're about to expose that knight. Kirsti, that wouldn't be very bright, would it? He had none of my own fierce competitiveness. Indeed, on this occasion, it almost seemed as if he did not want to be the victor because, for some obscure reason, he felt himself to be unworthy of victory.

When, after a whole series of rash moves from which he had been unable to deflect her, Kirsti said, 'That's it, I'd better resign,' he looked so regretful that anyone might have assumed that it was he who had lost.

'Yes, I think you'd better,' he agreed with a smile.

'A return?'

He lay back on the pillows. 'No. I think I'll turn in now.' When Kirsti involuntarily looked at her watch, he said, 'Yes, I know. It's terribly early. You and Rupert don't have to turn in yet. Why don't you go out and amuse yourselves?'

'Amuse ourselves?' Kirsti laughed. 'How does one amuse oneself in a town like this at this hour?'

'You could have a walk.'

'Yes, I suppose we could.'

I got to my feet, folding the newspaper and placing it on the bedside table. 'Why not? Come on.' I do not know whether I already foresaw what would follow.

Outside there was a breeze, the first for many days, which had brought a reviving coolness to the scorched, parched town. Perhaps because of it, there seemed to be many more people in the street.

'Do you think there's a nightclub in Balram?' Kirsti asked, clearly in joke.

'Or a theatre? Or an opera house?'

'Well, there's certainly a cinema.' I pointed up the street, to where a string of flickering lights garlanded a poster of a young, heavily moustached man brandishing a sword above the head of a full-breasted woman on her knees before him.

After that we walked on in silence. I felt the tension growing, growing, growing between us, even though, so far from touching each other, we each deliberately maintained a distance. Then I could stand it no longer. I gripped her arm roughly. 'Let's go back. I've had enough of this pointless wandering.'

She halted and we stood facing each other. 'We haven't wandered all that far,' she said in a weak, tremulous voice.

'Far enough. Come back to my room. He won't know.'

'But he'll have to know. Eventually.'

'Why should he?'

By then I knew, with a mounting excitement, that, yes, she would come up to my room.

Again we were silent as we retraced our steps. Kirsti's head was bowed and the skin of her face was glistening and pale, as though she were about to succumb to a fever like my father's. I put a hand on her shoulder, but at once she moved away. Was she afraid that someone — Rajiv perhaps — would see the contact and report it to my father? Was she about to change her mind?

'You are back early,' Mr Solomon said, as I asked him for my key.

'Yes, it's been a long day. We soon began to feel tired.'

'This heat is tiring for people not used to it.'

'What can it be like during the hot weather?'

Mr Solomon guffawed, his pendant jowls shaking. 'The hot weather is not for you.'

Throughout all this, Kirsti had been waiting patiently behind me.

She walked slowly, with a kind of sorrowful reluctance, along the corridor, up the concrete stairway and then along another corridor, heavy with the odour of curry, that would take us to my room. I unlocked the door, she went in ahead of me. 'They've been at it again,' I said. Then I explained, since she seemed not to understand. 'Next door. Cooking. God knows how many of them there are in there. I've seen three adults go in and out, and two — or is it three? — children.' In the years ahead I should always associate the smell of curry, pervading the room as well as the corridor, with all that then followed.

Kirsti seemed not to hear me as she stood by the bed, a hand to the top button of her blouse. It was as if she did not know what to say or do next. Then she crossed to the window and looked out and down, to the shadowy forecourt, full of broken-down old cars. She turned. 'What are we doing?'

'You know what we're doing. And that we both want to do it. Finis.' I walked decisively over to her and put my arms around her.

'How are we going to tell Philip?'

She had asked that question before. I made no answer, since I had none.

Breakfast is the best of all meals in India, just as the early morning is the best of all times. One of the boys, who could not have been more than thirteen or fourteen – there was an incipient moustache along his upper lip – brought in the tray. It contained scrambled eggs on toast, with three rashers of bacon, toast wrapped in what appeared to be Kleenex tissue, butter, marmalade in a glass saucer, and a metal pot of strong, bitter tea, with hot milk, skin wrinkled on its surface, in a metal jug. I sat with the tray on my bed. I felt voracious. I felt an edgy depression. I felt a tranquil happiness. The last two emotions might be thought to be mutually exclusive, but oddly they then existed side by side within me.

I wondered, as so often, what Kirsti and my father were doing at that moment. I wondered whether, in the state of tearful guilt in which she had left my room, she had blurted out something to him. If she had not done that, I wondered how, eventually, she and I would make our confession. That a confession would have to be made had been agreed by both of us. In the dark, stuffy little room, with the air-conditioner humming away ineffectually above us, Kirsti had made the momentous statement: 'I'm fond of him, I'm terribly fond of the poor dear. But it's all been a mistake.' Once again she had used that adjective 'poor'. But surely it was we, rather than my father, who were poor, I had thought without saying it to her. It was we who were impoverished both in loyalty and in the courage to tell the truth.

My breakfast over, I walked down the echoing corridor to the staircase that would take me down that other echoing corridor that would take me to their room. I wished that there were telephones in our rooms to enable us to communicate other than face to face. Somehow, after what had happened, it would be easier to speak to my father at that remove.

To my astonishment, he was up and dressed. Kirsti sat at the dressing-table behind him, making up her face.

'Father! This *is* a surprise!' My voice sounded horribly false to me.

His skin was grey, his shoulders slumped. Beads of sweat glistened on his upper lip, even though, unlike my room, their room was now cool.

'While you were still out last night, I had this bout of sweating. My sheet was soaked. And then, at the close of it, I knew I'd sweated out whatever bug it was. Kirsti took my temperature on her return and it was subnormal. I still feel weak, of course, but clearly I've recovered.'

'Oh, I'm so glad.'

He gave a small smile, as he sank, in apparent exhaustion, onto the end of his bed. 'Well, I had to recover, hadn't I? Think how much extra money we'd have had to spend to cancel our existing arrangements and fly back later, and how much inconvenience we'd have caused to others and ourselves. Now I'll be able to go to the cemetery.'

I was about to remind him that we were insured against any extra expenses due to illness. But Kirsti had looked round from the dressing-table. 'Today? You plan to go to the

[125]

cemetery today?' Until this moment, she had seemed to be deliberately protracting the process of making up her face in order not to have to look at me.

My father nodded. 'This morning. I've been busy already. While you were having your bath, I sent a message to Rajiv and also rang the Canadian mission from the lobby.'

'You rang the Canadian mission from the lobby?'

'Yes. I thought I'd like to see the Vellacotts again. I spoke to some girl, Canadian I suppose. They were due back from Delhi by the night train. She suggested going round sometime after ten. They have their brunch then. She seemed to be sure they'd want to see us. I don't know how she could be sure, since she's never met us and knows nothing about us.'

'Europeans must now be rare in Balram. I should think that any European visitor is welcome.' Kirsti had swivelled round on her stool before the dressing-table, a hairbrush in her hand. Our eyes linked, separated. A slow blush began to spread upwards from her neck, over her cheeks, to her forehead. In the past, it had always entertained and touched me to see her blush, like a young girl, over the most trivial things. But now that blush intensified my unease.

'You've had your breakfast?'

'Ages ago.' It was my father who answered the question. 'I've been awake since shortly before six. Kirsti woke later. Everyone gets up early in India, so one might as well do what everyone does.' But even in England my father always got up early, tapping away at his typewriter until the sound roused anyone else in the house.

Rajiv, waiting for us in the lobby, seemed to stare first at me and then at Kirsti with a hostile intentness, as my father exchanged a few jolly words not with Mr Solomon — he was not yet on duty — but with the tall, moustached young man who was his deputy. Or did I, raw with guilt, imagine that?

It was strange that I should be thinking about guilt, because, as we descended the stairs to the lobby, my father, having linked his arm in mine for support in his state of weakness, said, 'I feel guilty about the Vellacotts. All these years and I've made no attempt to get in touch with them, not even when we were making our plans to come out here. I didn't know if they were still in Balram, I didn't even know if they were alive or dead. Mackenzie has gone, so I gather. At least Solomon knows of no one of that name at the mission.'

I almost told him then of the grave beside my mother's. But Kirsti and I were not supposed to have gone to the cemetery without him. He had particularly asked us not to do so. Besides, I shrank from revealing to him one far distant truth, almost as much as I shrank from revealing to him another immediate one.

When we reached the mission, my father seemed to tumble rather than step out of the car. Stiffly he walked over to the front door, which was half open. There was a bell pull, at which he tugged. From within we could hear a hollow jangling.

An Indian servant padded up to the door. He looked in turn at the three of us with eyes red from weeping, lack of sleep or, perhaps, conjunctivitis.

'Good morning,' my father amiably greeted him. Then, when no reply was forthcoming, he asked, 'Is Mr Vellacott in?'

'Memsahib is here.'

We entered a hall panelled in pitch pine. I took in a carved teak chest, an elaborate Edwardian hatstand, and a chair with a high back covered in *petit point* of gaudy sunflowers on an emerald background.

'I will call memsahib.'

We looked at each other. Somewhere a clock began to chime. I counted — nine, ten, eleven, twelve. Clearly, since it was only a few minutes after ten, the clock was running slow or fast.

A sixtyish woman, in a khaki skirt and blouse, her legs bare, and old-fashioned, flat-heeled sandals on her feet, emerged through the door ahead of us. She had a table napkin in one hand, which she raised to dab at a corner of her mouth. Behind her was a dark-haired, dark-skinned girl, with a wide mouth and spectacles.

'Yes?' the woman said, peering through the gloom of the hall, in which all the blinds were lowered. Then her eyes fixed on my father. She let out a cry, 'Oh, my goodness!'

My father stepped forward. 'You remember me, Sybil?'

'Yes, of course I do. Of course!' She stepped towards him eagerly, to take his hand in both her own. Then, on an impulse, so it seemed, she leant forward and kissed him on the cheek. She swivelled round to look at me. Clearly she was puzzled. 'And this — is this . . . ?'

'This is Rupert. You remember Rupert, don't you?'

'Rupert! Yes, of course, I remember Rupert. He used to come up here to play with our Clive — or Clive would go down to you. What a pair of little monkeys they were!' Once again she appraised me. 'You've grown up different from what I'd expected.'

'I hope it's not too much of a shock!'

Taking my facetiousness literally, she gave a vigorous shake to her head, so that her bell of straight, pepper-and-salt hair, cut short below the ears and in a fringe in front, swung from side to side. 'Come and have some brunch with us. Enid said someone English had phoned. But she got the name all mixed up. Didn't you, dear?' She turned to the girl behind her, who gave a small, nervous smile, little more than a twitch of the mouth. 'She said a Mr Ryan, and I couldn't think who that might be. By the way, this is Enid, who helps us at the mission. She's priceless to us, I don't know how we'd manage without her.'

We all shook hands with Enid, who was clearly flustered by our attention. Since she spoke with a Canadian accent, I assumed that she had been educated there.

Mrs Vellacott motioned with a hand. 'Come into the dining room. You must try some of the honey from our bees.'

'I remember that honey,' my father said. 'You remember it, don't you, Rupert? You used to gorge yourself on it.' But I had no recollection of either the honey or Mrs Vellacott, although I remembered so many other things so clearly.

'You haven't introduced me,' Kirsti reminded my father, as we gathered round the oval mahogany table, a lazy-susan, laden with honey, jams, pickles, and a butter dish in its middle. It had struck me as odd that my father, usually so punctilious about such things, had made this omission. From time to time Mrs Vellacott had been stealing surreptitious glances at Kirsti, as though puzzled as to who she might be.

'Nor I have! This is my wife, Kirsti.'

'Your wife!' She could not keep the astonishment out of her voice. 'I thought that perhaps . . .' She broke off. It was all too clear to Kirsti and me, and perhaps also to my father, what she had thought. She had thought Kirsti to be my wife or my girlfriend. 'Then you married again.'

'Yes. A few months ago. Kirsti comes from Finland.'

'I've never been to Finland. Noel went there once. Some conference of the World Council of Churches. We couldn't both afford to go. . . . Do please sit down. Anywhere. No compliments.'

'Where is Noel?' my father asked, pulling back a chair.

'He was coming back with me. But then the bishop wanted him to stay on for an extra day. They had so many things to discuss. I couldn't stay, we have a meeting of our mothers. This afternoon.' She turned to Kirsti. 'It might interest you. You could talk to them. They'd love that.'

Kirsti smiled, uncertain how to reply. It was my father who rescued her, with one of his rare fibs. 'We're planning to drive out to the fort this afternoon. Otherwise, I'm sure Kirsti would have been delighted to accept.'

Through all this the girl Enid was looking eagerly from one of our faces to the other.

'What a spread!' my father exclaimed.

'Well, you may remember how we've always lived. No change. We get up extremely early, just like the Indians, and we have our *chotah hazri*. Then, between ten and eleven, we have our brunch. And in the evening, early in the evening, we have our dinner — or supper.'

'We've already had our breakfast,' Kirsti said.

'Well, never mind. Try one of these scones. I made them myself. Wholemeal flour.'

Politely Kirsti refused. My father put out a hand and took one, then whirled the lazy-susan around in order to get at the butter. 'I've been ill,' he said. 'This is the first day I've felt well for, oh, almost a week. It's also the first day I've had any appetite.'

'Oh, I do wish you'd telephoned to tell me. I might have been able to be of help.'

'We had an excellent doctor. Dr da Costa. Mr Solomon at the hotel got hold of him.'

'Yes, I know Dr da Costa. His father and mother, both now dead, were part of our flock. Sadly, he's no longer one of us.

But he's a good man, a thoroughly good man — and an excellent doctor.' She picked up the knife and fork from the plate before her and resumed eating what was, by now, a congealed fried egg beside a curl of bacon. Munching, she said, 'How did we ever lose touch with each other?'

My father was spreading honey thickly on his scone. 'Well, we corresponded for a brief while, didn't we?'

She laughed, showing butter-coloured teeth in her plain, friendly face. 'For a very short time! Two letters, three letters? Well, we could understand it. In those circumstances. As Noel said, it was natural that you'd want to forget the terrible thing that happened here.'

My father, staring down at the half-eaten scone in his hand, suddenly looked abstracted and humbled. 'Yes,' he said in a low, hoarse voice, almost as though his laryngitis had returned. 'I wanted to forget.' Then he looked up. 'But there was also the war. That came soon after, of course. I was swept into the RAF, shot down, taken prisoner. After I got back . . .' His voice faded.

'Oh, we *perfectly* understood.' And, indeed, Mrs Vellacott was clearly the sort of decent, kind, tolerant woman who would bear no grudges for neglect and ingratitude, whatever their reasons. She leant across the table to Kirsti. 'Do please have *something* to eat. Why not some fruit? These apples really are very good. They come from the hills, of course, they don't grow here.'

Kirsti took an apple. I knew that she did not really want it, she was eating from politeness. I, too, would have to do my duty. I put out a hand and took one of the scones.

'After we've left you, we're going to the cemetery to see Irene's grave. That's really why we came here. Balram really has nothing to offer to the tourist, has it?' Once again, innocent of all desire to wound, my father had come out with something that might easily do so.

But Mrs Vellacott did not take the remark amiss. 'Yes, it's a backwater,' she agreed. 'But Noel and I have come to love it, we'd not want to be anywhere else. As long as the mission allows us to stay here, we will. I expect that, in due course, we'll also make the journey up to our little cemetery for the last time.' She smiled round at us. Clearly the prospect did not alarm or depress her. 'That cemetery,' she went on, rotating the lazy-susan, 'I'm afraid you'll find it's become very sad. Once the English went . . . Our funds are dwindling and it seems to us more important to spend the little that we have on the living than on the dead.' She was carefully scraping an exiguous amount of butter across the surface of a scone. 'But I do try to care for Irene's grave. I go up from time to time to do that.'

Suddenly my father looked so contrite, like some child caught out in some misdemeanour, that I thought he might burst into tears. His hands, with the purple-corded veins on their backs, gripped the edge of the table, as he stared down at them. 'I ought . . . I ought . . . Should have sent some money . . . Upkeep.' He did no more than mumble. 'Just that I . . . wanted to put it all . . . out of my mind for ever.' We all, even Enid, watched him in embarrassment. 'But of course I couldn't. One can't. It's all there.'

Mrs Vellacott broke the silence that followed. 'First you went, then Claud moved to Calcutta and someone we never really liked took over on the railway. We felt very lonely then. Oh, how we missed you.' She raised her cup of tea in both her hands, her plain face suddenly impressive in its stillness and sadness. 'And Jack Mackenzie dying,' she added. 'That was heartbreaking. Such a wonderful man, such a wonderful

[132]

doctor.' One could tell that the sorrow of his loss was still vivid to her. 'It almost broke our hearts. We thought of him as a son.'

My father was staring at her, his mouth half open and his eyelids blinking as though to hold back a weight of unshed tears. 'He *died*?'

She nodded mournfully. 'Yes. Didn't you know? I thought you must have known.'

Mutely my father shook his head. He had become so extraordinarily pale that, for a moment, I feared that he was again going to collapse, as he had done in the lobby of the hotel. 'How did he die?' he looked up at last to ask.

'Tuberculosis. Like poor dear Irene. What a toll that disease took! No one now remembers. The white plague, that's what they used to call it, didn't they? You'd never have imagined that a man so healthy and athletic, so full of life, would have succumbed to it. But he did. In a matter of months. Miliary tuberculosis, galloping consumption. That was the worst form.'

'Poor Mackenzie.' My father muttered it.

Again there was that tense silence around the table. To relieve it, I asked, 'What happened to his bungalow?'

'Oh, his bungalow!' Clearly I had touched on something else unhappy. 'Well, you remember he had that little consulting room there. He was so wonderful, treating the poorest people, outcasts, for nothing, nothing at all. Well, after he died, we had this idea that, as a memorial to him, we'd build this little hospital that had always been his dream. We collected some money, but no one around here has much, and then the maharajah promised us some more, a lot more. We had the bungalow pulled down, we had an architect from Indore, an absolutely brilliant man, draw up some designs. He

[133]

was a Christian, so he wouldn't charge anything, not a single *anna*. The mission promised to send us another medical man. We even laid the foundations, the bishop came over for that. And then . . . then . . . Well, the British left, and the maharajah lost a lot of his estates and . . . Well, we never blamed him. It wasn't really his fault, though I suppose . . . But it was a terrible disappointment to us.' She looked around the table at us. 'The money just wasn't there. So . . .' She shrugged her bony shoulders. 'No hospital, no bungalow. And no medical man to replace dear Jack.'

After that the conversation became more relaxed, with Mrs Vellacott talking first of the old maharani, then of my uncle, and then of people whom I had long since forgotten, if indeed I had ever known them. At one point Kirsti looked across the table to me. Her gaze said all too clearly: How long does this have to go on?

At long last my father rose to his feet, pushing back his chair so vigorously that it rucked up the kelim behind it. Enid stooped to pull it straight again. 'Well, we ought to be on our way to the cemetery,' he said.

Outside the front door, he took Mrs Vellacott's hand in his and then held it there. His eyes glittered. Was it a revival of grief or the brilliant sunshine after the indoors gloom that had caused the tears to form? I could not be sure. 'Thank you,' he said, clearly moved. 'Thank you,' he repeated, at a loss for words. Then he went on, 'You were so kind to us then. And, without my knowing it, you've gone on being so kind to us.'

His emotion had clearly communicated itself to our hostess. 'Oh, nonsense! What have I done? Some weeding, some planting. That's all. I loved her, you know. She was such a sweet, gentle, *good* creature.' She thought for a moment, her face veiled by grief. 'Jack too. So *good*.'

Slumped silent in his seat beside Rajiv, my father seemed strangely abject. Was he still consumed with guilt for having neglected both my mother's grave and the Vellacotts for so many years? Or was there some even darker cause? From time to time he let out a deep sigh. At each, Rajiv would glance across at him with concern.

Eventually Kirsti leant forward, once again putting that strong, competent hand on his shoulder. 'What's the matter?'

'Nothing, nothing.' With that childish fretfulness that was the nearest he ever came to rage, he shook his head from side to side. Then he muttered, 'Horrible town. Horrible, horrible town.'

'Oh, it's not so bad,' Kirsti said with a laugh. 'I've got used to it. I've almost begun to like it.'

'We spent five months here, and with each day I hated it more and more.'

'Well, there was a reason for that,' she told him.

My father had never before said that he had hated Balram. Indeed, on the rare occasions when he had spoken to me of the place, it had been with the same indulgent fondness with which he spoke of the rest of India.

The car drew up under the tamarind trees, beside the high gates. The truck that had been continuously hooting behind us for minutes on end, now hurtled past, covering us in dust. Kirsti put a handkerchief to her mouth.

'Why are we stopping here?' my father turned to Rajiv to ask.

'This is the cemetery, sahib.' Rajiv was looking at him with mournful pity.

'*This?* But this can't be it. This must be another cemetery.' He leant across Rajiv and peered out. I did not dare to say: *This is the cemetery, father. Kirsti and I came here yesterday. I've even seen mother's grave.* Then, his eyes on the gates, he slowly took it in. 'But how could everything have changed so much?' He seemed to be struggling to achieve not merely a physical but a spiritual reorientation. For a long time he continued to stare at the gates, while the three of us watched him. 'This was all country before!' he cried out in repressed anguish. 'That's how I've always remembered it. As open country.' That was how he had always described it to me, and therefore how I, too, had remembered it until we had first entered Balram. 'How could this have happened?'

'You've seen for yourself how the whole of Balram has changed,' I reminded him.

'But not *this!*' He bowed his head. Again he began to mutter, to himself, not to us. I caught: 'Factories . . . smoke . . . noise . . .'

I began to get out of the car. 'Well, now that we're here, we'd better have a look.'

'Yes, of course, of course.' He pushed open the door beside him and stepped out, almost into a ditch. Stones, loosened by his feet, cascaded downwards, as he gripped the door handle to prevent himself from falling.

'Take care!' Kirsti cried out.

Rajiv went round the car to help him, taking him solicitously by the arm. 'This way, sahib. No, not there. Step here. Here, please.' He might have been talking to a blind man.

'Don't get out that side, Kirsti,' I told her. 'You might be less lucky and slip into that ditch. God knows what horrors are in it.'

Kirsti began to shift herself across the seat towards me, where I stood holding the door open for her. Then, when she had reached its end, she swung out her smooth, brown legs, and extended her hand for me to take. Her face, as she did so, was suddenly illuminated by an extraordinary happiness, as though, down through a leaden sky, a shaft of sunlight had suddenly caressed me. For a moment we seemed to be immobilized, her glowing face upturned to mine and mine downturned to hers, our hands clasped. Then she wriggled further forward, I gave her hand a tug, and she was out beside me.

I turned. Rajiv and my father, standing close to each other as though in mutual defence, were staring at us. Rajiv's eyes had in them a frigid, fastidious contempt that I had never seen in them before. That shocked me. But what shocked me even more was the clammy, stretched pallor of the skin around my father's mouth and his anguished, grieving eyes. He looked far worse than he had at the mission. Kirsti glanced over to me and raised her eyebrows and her shoulders almost imperceptibly.

My father turned away. 'Well, we'd better get started.'

'Are you sure you feel equal to it?' Kirsti asked.

'Perfectly.'

As my father walked off, Rajiv attempted to take his arm. Brutally he pulled free. 'No, no. I'm all right. Perfectly capable of taking a little walk.'

In single file, my father in the lead, then Rajiv, then Kirsti and finally myself, we made our way up the narrow corridor of graves overgrown with moss and creepers. As on my previous visit, the sound of the invisible cicadas, throbbing all about us, eventually seemed to become a pulse within my own body, so agonizing in its insistence that I could hardly stand it.

Bare feet pattered behind us. Turning, I saw an Indian whom I took to be the custodian of the place. Breathless from his pursuit, he first saluted us, legs straight and hands to his sides, as though he were a soldier confronted by some members of the General Staff, and then asked us which grave we wished to see.

Unthinking, I all but blurted out that I had visited the cemetery before, that I knew my way about it, that I had found the grave for which we were bound. But luckily, before I could do so, my father had spoken.

As soon as he had heard the name, the custodian raced ahead of us, hopping from one grave to another, as though they were stepping stones, while he called out shrilly, 'Come, come, come,' and flapped his long arms. He might have been some giant bird. Then he turned and halted, smiling to reveal the few teeth stuck like burnt-out matches in his purple gums. 'Vellacott memsahib come often. I help.' Then he hurried on again, pausing from time to time to look over his shoulder to see that we were still following.

Where the gentle slope reached a grassy summit, the sky was again lurid with smoke from the nearby factory. Beneath the crackling of the cicadas, I could now hear, eerily close, the roar of the traffic, as I had not been able to do when first we had left the road.

I had overtaken my father and passed him. When I waited for him to catch up with me — Kirsti trailed, seemingly intentionally, far behind us — he put out a hand to grip my arm, just above the wrist, as though to steady himself on some steep ascent. 'All changed. Unrecognizable.' It was as though he were talking not only of the cemetery and not only of Balram but of his past life. 'One wouldn't have thought it possible.'

The guardian was once again standing, like a soldier to attention, before the grave which I already knew to be my mother's. As my father, with Rajiv and me behind him, came

[138]

up to the grave, he stepped smartly to one side for us and then, like a guide at a museum, held out an arm to point. 'Here is lady,' he said, his voice swelling with triumph at having brought us unerringly to our destination.

Rajiv and I halted. My father stepped forward. Head bowed, he went up to the grave and then, with an odd infolding of his body on itself, head going forward first, he knelt down beside it. He put a hand out to the stone for support, then moved the hand over its surface, as though testing its smoothness. His face was blank, withdrawn. I wondered what emotions were throbbing within him, like the sounds of the cicadas all about us, what terrible music, at long last unfrozen, was reaching a tumultuous crescendo.

He remained there a long time, head bowed and hand now motionless in its inertness on the stone of the grave. I looked round for Kirsti. Perhaps feeling that she must not intrude on this communication between him and his dead first wife, she was standing some distance away, under the shadow of the riven angel. I could not see her face clearly, but I sensed a tension in her whole waiting stance.

When my father at last got up off his knees, Rajiv hurried forward to put out a hand to help him. But again my father rejected this act of tenderness – which I myself should have performed, I see clearly now – with unnecessary and uncharacteristic brusqueness. He straightened, looked about him. I knew that, sooner or later, he would notice the other grave, however much I willed him not to do so.

As though he had known of its existence all along and had only not acknowledged it sooner in order to give all his initial attention to my mother's, he slowly crossed over to it. This time he did not kneel. He merely gazed down at the simple, bold inscription, his lips moving almost imperceptibly, in the

[139]

manner of a child, as he read it over to himself.

'Mackenzie sahib,' the custodian said unnecessarily.

'Mackenzie sahib?' Rajiv repeated the word on an upward inflection as though to ask a question.

'Here.' My father seemed to utter the monosyllable not to me, not to Rajiv or the custodian, not even to himself, but to the spirit of this dry, hot, forlorn place. He gave himself a visible shake, as though in an agonizing effort to reassemble within him the jagged shards of a kaleidoscope. Then he smiled at me with an extraordinary sweetness and, in a gesture of tenderness such as he had never before shown to me in the whole course of my life, he put a hand to my cheek and caressed it for a moment. 'So that's that.'

He walked ahead of me to Kirsti, who still stood waiting, with what communicated itself to me as a terrible agitation, under the shadow of the angel. He put out both his hands to her, as though in joyous welcome. At first reluctantly, then with clumsy eagerness, she took them in hers. He turned, still holding her hands in his, and waited for me to join them.

As I came up, uncertain and panicky, he took the two hands that he had been clasping and moved them towards me, as though he were making me a present of something infinitely precious. Again he gave me that smile of extraordinary sweetness, but now it was tinged with an even more extraordinary sadness.

I took the hands in my own.

He turned his back on us and then moved off, raising his right hand in what appeared to be a final valediction.

I realized then that there were no secrets of the past and no secrets of the present that I had to divulge to him. He had apprehended them all already.

FOUR

*H*E IS SITTING OUT in his wheelchair at the far end of the garden below my study window. There is a tartan rug over his knees and a book is lying, face downwards, on the long grass which, for days now, I have been telling myself, and Kirsti has been telling me, that I must mow. The grass makes a gentle sea around him. He is sleeping, as he so often sleeps now, and the sun has retreated, leaving him in the shade. *Nox ruit, Aenea.* Shadows of the evening steal across the sky. There are so many tasks to be done in the garden in which he sleeps on, and now he will do none of them.

Below my study is the smaller, tidier study that Kirsti and I made for him from the old nursery, when, having refused to go into a home ('A home is not a home'), he had at last agreed to come and live with us. On the desk, there is the old Remington typewriter, taken out to India with my mother before the war. There are box files, a card index, an array of pens and pencils. There is even a half-covered page about the architecture of the palace at Indore. But though he may wheel himself into this study, and though he may even open one or other of the files, turning over pages creased and yellow from age and staring down at them with those still bright, still eager eyes of his, nothing, nothing at all will ever be completed. Only last night, suddenly introspective, he said with a sigh, 'All my life is nothing but loose ends.'

I thought then, as I think now, of those loose ends that he so heroically, so decisively and so magnanimously tied together in the cemetery in Balram, with that eloquent gesture of transferring Kirsti's hands from his own into mine. But I could not speak of it to him, I cannot speak of it to him now.

I go out of my study and call down the stairwell. 'Kirsti! Kirsti!'

She is watching television with the youngest of our three children.

'Yes!' she calls back. Unlike me, she is never exasperated at being disturbed in what she is doing.

'I think you'd better bring him in. The sun is leaving the garden.'

Why do I not go down and bring him in myself?

I stand at the window and watch her as she walks, with that strong, elegant, still youthful carriage of hers, out over the sea of long grass.

He opens his eyes at her approach. He looks up at her. He smiles. He smiles with a still radiant, still welcoming, still forgiving love.